CAVE-IN

Linda moved slowly through the cave, shining the light on both sides, looking for any place where a deed could have been left.

This is it—I've gone far enough, Linda decided. She turned and started the slow, crouching walk back toward the entrance. Outside, Amber whinnied.

"Calm down, Amber, I'm coming," Linda called. But her words were drowned out by a deep rumbling in the tunnel.

A timber overhead cracked. Rocks and dirt showered down. Linda reached forward in the darkness to find a huge boulder completely blocking her escape.

She was trapped!

THE LINDA CRAIG ADVENTURES™ #1

THE GOLDEN SECRET

By Ann Sheldon

A MINSTREL® BOOK

PUBLISHED BY POCKET BOOKS

New York   London   Toronto   Sydney   Tokyo

A MINSTREL PAPERBACK *ORIGINAL*

 A Minstrel Book published by
POCKET BOOKS, a division of Simon & Schuster, Inc.,
1230 Avenue of the Americas, New York, N.Y. 10020

ISBN: 0-671-64034-8

First Minstrel Books printing May 1988

10 9 8 7, 6 5 4 3 2 1

A MINSTREL BOOK and colophon are
registered trademarks of Simon & Schuster, Inc.

THE LINDA CRAIG ADVENTURES is a
trademark of Simon & Schuster, Inc.

LINDA CRAIG is a registered trademark
of Simon & Schuster, Inc.

Printed in the U.S.A.

THE GOLDEN SECRET

1 ♦♦♦♦

"You're the best horse in the world, Amber!" Linda Craig leaned down to pat Amber's silken mane. "And today we're going to prove it!"

Linda touched her heels to the sides of her golden palomino. Then, with a gentle pull on the reins, the twelve-year-old girl guided her horse out of the schooling ring and toward the stable.

Amber swung into a smooth and easy trot, perfectly following Linda's command. The mare seemed every bit as excited as Linda was. Linda had trained her horse for months, but today was the first time they'd be out on the trails of Rancho del Sol.

She slowed Amber as they came to the big oval corral beyond the stable. Then Linda leaped down off the horse and kissed her velvety nose.

"Come on, let's cool off." She pulled the reins over the horse's head and left them slack so Amber could relax as they walked.

Beyond the corral fence, Linda could see the trail she'd soon be riding. She and her older brother, Bob, had invited their best friends to explore the western end of the ranch. They would have a perfect day for it. The sun was brilliant in the sky, and recent rain had made the world smell new. Linda stopped and took a deep breath.

Amber nudged Linda's shoulder with her nose —she wanted to be scratched behind the ears. "You just can't get enough attention, can you?" Linda laughed as she reached up. Amber turned her head from side to side, helping Linda scratch all the right places.

Amber's long white forelock hid the star that splashed across her face. Still, Linda didn't want to cut any of the mare's thick snowy hair. It was one of the things that made her so beautiful.

As if reading Linda's thoughts, Amber ducked her head, letting her forelock flop over her eyes. Linda led her into the corral and turned her out with the other horses. Then, as Linda headed out of the corral, Amber darted forward. She snatched the brim of Linda's cowboy hat with her teeth, pulling it off.

"Hey!" Linda's dark hair whipped around her shoulders as she turned back to Amber. "Give that back." She tried to make her voice sound stern, but laughter lit up Linda's brown eyes as Amber shook her head, making the hat flap.

"Need a hat, lady?" a voice came from behind. Linda turned to see her brother grinning down at her. Bob plopped his own hat on her head and hopped over the corral fence. "You can borrow mine until I get yours back."

Bob headed for Amber, but the horse pranced around him, always staying a foot out of reach.

"Very funny." Bob's blue eyes were beginning to flash with anger as he ran a hand through his short blond hair. "Are you sure she's ready to go out on the trail?"

"She's just playful, that's all." Linda stepped forward and put her hand out. "No more playing, Amber," she said seriously.

The horse trotted up and dropped the hat in her hand. "You'll see how ready Amber is when we leave you behind in a cloud of dust!"

Bob laughed. "That'll be the day! You and a green little mare outrunning me and Rocket." Bob was fifteen, three years older than Linda, and to him, older definitely meant smarter. "By the way, Kathy called and said she'll be late, so Larry and I will meet you on the trail." He hefted a pack of sandwiches. "I'll carry the supplies. We don't want to overload poor Amber."

Before Linda could reply, they heard the sound of a horse's hooves pounding up the drive. They turned and saw Larry Spencer and his Appaloosa, Snowbird, galloping up in one of Larry's usual dramatic entrances. Snowbird was a solidly built horse, with dark forequarters and a splash of white markings on his rump.

"Well? Let's go!" Larry yelled. He always jumped into things, acting first and thinking about it later. Sometimes that got him and Bob into tight spots, but Larry's wits and quick smile kept them out of any real trouble. "There's a whole ranch out there, just waiting for us!"

He looked from Bob to Linda. "Aren't you ready yet? I thought we were going to have lunch in the foothills." He looked off toward the mountains to the west.

"We will, but Kathy is going to be late. I'll go pack some more stuff for lunch, and we'll meet you out at the south gate," Linda said.

The two boys headed toward the stable, and Linda walked back to the house. For her and Bob, Rancho del Sol was home—they'd lived on the ranch in Southern California with their grandparents, Doña and Bronco Mallory, since their parents had died in an accident.

As Linda came to the kitchen door, she could hear Luisa Alvarez singing inside. Small, dark-haired Luisa had come to Rancho del Sol as the housekeeper. But she had worked at the ranch for so long that now she was part of the family. She smiled as Linda came in. "Here are the brownies for your ride," she said.

"I hope they're not all for Linda," said Doña Mallory, stepping into the kitchen. "I like them, too."

Linda laughed. "I guess I'll have to share with Doña, Luisa."

Even though her real name was Rosalinda Mallory, everyone on the ranch called Linda's grandmother Doña. It was a Spanish title of respect, used before a woman's first name. But Doña Rosalinda was such a mouthful that it had been shortened to Doña.

No matter what she was called, Doña was an

amazing woman, who loved the ranch, its land, and its history. A superb horsewoman, she knew just about every foot of her family's property.

"Getting supplies for the big ride today?" Doña asked, smiling.

Linda nodded, wrapping up the sandwiches she'd made for herself and Kathy and adding some fruit.

Luisa tossed an apple to Linda. "You might as well take this for that horse of yours." In spite of her many years at the ranch, Luisa was afraid of horses. Yet she tried to understand Linda's love for Amber.

Linda finished packing the lunch and glanced up at the kitchen clock. What was taking Kathy so long?

Doña followed her eyes. "Look at the time," she said. "I'd better go change out of my riding clothes. Silas Danner called—he's coming over to discuss something with us."

She turned to Linda. "Would you please tell your grandfather to expect Mr. Danner? I'll be down in a few minutes."

Linda hurried through the house to her grandfather's study. That's where Bronco Mallory started his day, looking over the books and taking care of the business of managing Rancho del Sol. Linda found him sitting behind his desk, dressed as he usually was

6

in jeans and a western shirt with pearl buttons. Even when he had worked the range all day, Bronco somehow managed to look neat and well tailored. He looked up at Linda and grinned.

"What's up, honey?" he asked in his deep voice. "I thought you'd be off and riding by now."

"I would be—but I'm waiting for Kathy," Linda answered.

Bronco smiled. "Well, if Amber does as well on the trail as she does in the ring, you've got a winner there! And you've certainly worked hard. Just don't get overconfident. It's Amber's first time out. Even if you think she's solid gold, Amber is still a little green."

"Oh, Bronco," Linda said, but she promised to be careful. Then she gave him Doña's message.

"Danner, eh?" Bronco frowned in thought. "I wonder what he wants."

Silas Danner owned the biggest bank in Lockwood, the town nearest Rancho del Sol. Linda didn't really know Mr. Danner. She sure knew his grandson, though—and Eric Danner was a real pest. He was in the same class as Kathy and Linda, and somehow he always managed to cause trouble.

"I hope it's not this oil business again." Bronco

sighed. "He's been after us to start drilling on the ranch. There may be oil down there. *Maybe.*"

"I think it would be neat to have an oil well," said Linda. "It's like those gold mines that Doña's great-grandfather dug."

Bronco smiled. "There never was much gold in those mines, honey. And I won't go tearing up the ranch on a maybe. We do well enough with what's *on* Rancho del Sol without worrying about what's *under* it."

Linda nodded. She knew that Rancho del Sol was famous for its herd of Black Angus cattle—and the horses that Bronco raised.

The doorbell rang, and Bronco stood up. "That must be Silas now," he said. "Well, I guess we'll find out what he wants soon enough. Have a great ride, Linda!"

"Thanks," she said, heading back to the kitchen. As she came into the room, she saw Amber's head and shoulders framed in the top half of the doorway. The horse tossed her head up and down impatiently.

"No horses in the kitchen!" Luisa flapped her apron as if she were shooing hens.

Amber shook her head but didn't back away.

"You let yourself out of the corral again," Linda scolded Amber. "I hope you didn't get into any other mischief."

Luisa was watching Amber nervously, but Linda laughed. "Don't worry, Luisa. Amber is smart enough to unlatch the corral gate, but she hasn't figured out kitchen doors yet."

Taking some lumps of sugar from the bowl on the table, Linda opened the door. "Let's go, Amber. I'll take you back to the corral and we can meet Kathy there." Amber crunched one lump of sugar, then nuzzled Linda's jeans pocket for more as she followed her.

Someone had already closed the corral gate, so Linda went into the stable and got her tack. Amber followed and stood patiently while Linda put a saddle on her and tightened the cinch. After Linda had carefully checked that everything was just right and that Amber was comfortable, she swung into the saddle. She had to duck her head as they rode out of the stable.

At the corner of the stable, Linda saw Mac, the ranch foreman, waiting for her. His long, lanky form leaned against the hitching rail, and he was chewing on a straw as if he had nothing to do. But Bronco always said that Mac did more work than any other three men.

"That horse of yours had a good time," Mac drawled. "She tore open the feed bales and left hay all over, which *I* had to clean up."

"I'm sorry, Mac." Although he sounded stern, Linda could see the twinkle in his deep-set blue eyes. Mac was Linda and Bob's best friend on Rancho del Sol. Mac had taught them how to ride and rope, and they trusted him with their secrets. "Next time I'll loop a piece of wire from the gate to the post. She can't undo that," Linda promised.

"Wouldn't count on it." There was a smile in Mac's eyes. Linda knew he was almost as fond of Amber as she was. "By the way, I saw somebody riding up the drive."

"Thanks, Mac," Linda called, heading Amber toward the driveway that wound past the house and eventually joined the road.

Amber pricked her ears forward and nickered when she saw Kathy Hamilton trotting toward them on her pinto, Patches.

"Sorry I'm so late. Mom needed help this morning." Kathy tried to straighten out her wind-tangled blond hair. "But she sent along cookies as a peace offering."

"Luisa gave me some brownies, too. I packed them—oh no! I left our lunch back in the kitchen! Hold on a second."

Linda turned Amber and, with a gentle kick, urged her into a trot. At the house Linda dismounted and ground-tied Amber by dropping the reins to the ground.

As Linda walked into the kitchen, she heard angry voices coming from the living room. She peeked through the doorway, to see Mr. Danner standing in front of her grandparents.

"This is impossible!" Doña angrily jumped up from the sofa. "There must be some mistake."

"It's no mistake," Silas Danner said, shaking his head. "And it's not impossible. *You're going to lose Rancho del Sol!*"

2 ♦♦♦♦

"Maybe you'd better explain yourself, Silas." Bronco rose to his feet.

Linda stood frozen in the doorway, watching.

"Well, let's put it this way. Who owns this ranch?" Mr. Danner said.

Doña laughed. "Silas, you know as well as I do, this ranch has been my family's for more than a hundred years."

"I know that's how it seemed, but the facts may be a little different."

"What facts?" Bronco's voice was dangerously quiet.

"Seems there's some difficulty about the title," Mr. Danner said. "My clients own a cattle company up in

Los Angeles, and they're buying up ranch land around here."

Doña cut him off. "Rancho del Sol has never been for sale."

Linda could tell how angry Doña was from the tilt of her grandmother's chin.

"Look," Silas Danner said. "This is prime land. My clients are mighty anxious to get hold of it. They asked me to check it out and see how things stood. Just out of curiosity I thought I'd take a look at the deed." He paused.

For a moment no one spoke. Linda could feel her heart pounding.

"That should have settled it," Bronco said.

"Not quite."

Linda could hear the triumph in Mr. Danner's voice.

"It seems there's no proof of ownership in the county records. None at all."

"There must be some mistake," Bronco said. "Don Carlos Perez would have filed a claim of ownership when he started ranching here. Sometimes they were casual about legalities in those days, but not that casual."

"There's no mistake." Mr. Danner's voice sharpened. "I made a thorough search. There's no trace of a deed."

"Of course not," Doña said. "The original records were destroyed in the courthouse fire while Don Carlos was still alive."

"Then he must have refiled, using his copy of the deed," Bronco said.

"No, he didn't," Mr. Danner said. "There is no record whatever."

"It wasn't necessary," Doña said.

"The law thinks otherwise. If Don Carlos failed to reregister ownership and the original deed can't be produced, the land reverts to the state. The company I represent has big money. They can buy the place right out from under you. It's not pretty, but it's the truth."

"Now, hold on a minute," Bronco said angrily. "You can't just barge in here and tell us this ranch doesn't belong to us."

"I'm just telling you about the law." Danner's voice was cool. "And suggesting that maybe you should accept a good price for the ranch—now."

"This ranch is my heritage," Doña said. "Nobody can take it from me."

"We'll fight you on this," Bronco said grimly.

"According to my lawyers, you'll lose. Think about my suggestion. At least you'll get something for the ranch." Silas Danner turned and strode out of the house. Linda heard him march to his car, get in, and slam the door. Then he took off so quickly the tires tossed gravel into the air.

"Well," Bronco was saying. "That was a shocker."

"We'll just have to fight it." Doña sounded fierce. "Bronco, let's call our lawyers and tell them we're coming over. I can promise Silas Danner one thing —we're going to keep Rancho del Sol."

Linda realized she'd been holding her breath. She let it out in a sigh. If Doña and Bronco were that determined, somehow things would turn out all right.

Then she heard the clop of a horse's hooves coming up the drive to the house. It must be Kathy, Linda thought, coming to see what's keeping me. She grabbed the lunches and ran out the kitchen door.

"Linda, you're as white as a sheet!" Kathy gasped. "What's the matter?"

"Wait till I tell you what I just overheard!" Linda put the food into her saddlebags, checked Amber's girth, and swung into the saddle. "Let's catch up to

15

the guys and I'll fill everyone in at once. Let's go!" she shouted. "Race you to the south pasture."

Linda squeezed her calves to Amber's sides, and the horse jumped forward as if some tightly coiled spring had been released. Linda felt her own heart leap with excitement.

She meant to look back to see if Patches was keeping up, but the thrill of racing across the fields on Amber's back soon put everything else completely out of Linda's mind.

Amber never slowed down as they approached the pasture where Bob and Larry were supposed to meet them. Then she responded smoothly and quickly when Linda reined her in.

Linda was so happy with Amber that at first she didn't even notice that the boys weren't there.

"What a run!" she said. "And you're barely breathing hard!" She wrapped her arms around the horse's neck.

Amber turned her head and tried to catch Linda's sleeve in her teeth. Linda dug out another lump of sugar from her pocket.

"I'd better get you hooked on carrots, or you'll get fat with all this sugar." She straightened up. "Now, where are those guys?"

Kathy and Patches came pounding up. Patches' hooves thumped roughly into the ground as he galloped. His sides were heaving.

"Wow, that Amber!" Kathy said. "You looked as if you were floating."

Linda nodded. "She really has a smooth gait." Then she looked around. "Wouldn't you know, those guys didn't wait."

"Look, they left a note." Kathy pointed to a small piece of paper that fluttered from a sharpened twig stuck into the ground.

Linda slid off her horse and went to look. "It's a message, all right. It says: 'Slowpokes. Meet you at Picnic Cave.' He means that old cave near the little pond."

Kathy nodded. "Okay, let's go. I'm hungry. Did you bring tons of food? I brought corn chips, cookies, and soft drinks." She pulled up her horse's head. "Hey, Patches. We're not at the picnic yet. No eating grass with a bit in your mouth."

Patches looked bored.

Linda climbed back into the saddle and led the way, riding more slowly for Kathy's sake. She was bursting to tell her about Mr. Danner's visit, but she decided to wait until they caught up with the

17

boys. Then she wouldn't have to tell everything twice.

As they came up over a rise in the land, the girls saw Bob and Larry. Bob was leaning toward Larry as he pointed to a truck parked a short distance away. Slowing the horses to a walk, Linda and Kathy went over to them.

"Did your grandfather get a new truck?" Kathy asked as they joined the boys.

"No. I've never seen it before," Bob said.

"Well, let's find out what it's doing here." Linda started toward the pickup.

The two men alongside the truck were busy stowing some kind of equipment in the back. They were rugged-looking men in jeans, work shirts, and dark glasses. One of them wore a baseball cap. He glanced up at the four riders, then went back to work.

Bob rode out in front. "Hi," he said. "Can we help you? Are you lost?"

The bigger man said, "Nope," and got into the pickup on the driver's side. The second man placed some tools in the back. He wore his cap pulled down over his eyes.

"What's all this?" Larry rode close and leaned down to touch what looked like a pump of some kind.

The man swung his arm up and knocked Larry's hand away.

"Hey!" Larry said.

"Keep your hands off what doesn't belong to you, son."

Linda moved Amber closer. "We don't like to be unfriendly," she said, "but *you're* on land that doesn't belong to you."

"Is that so?" The man drawled the words unpleasantly. He put his hand flat on Amber's shoulder and tried to push her back so he could get into the truck on the passenger side. Amber didn't budge. The man muttered something and pushed past the horse, having to squeeze against the truck's side to get by. He got into the pickup and slammed the door. The driver gunned the engine, then took off in a burst of speed.

"Well!" Bob said. "What do you suppose that was all about?"

"Good thing that guy didn't try to shove Snowbird," Larry said. "He'd have gone home without one of his fingers." Snowbird was not the best-natured horse in the world.

"But who were they and what were they doing?" Kathy said.

"I don't know. But I got the number on their license plate," Linda said. She repeated it to herself a few times to fix it in her memory.

"Their tracks come from the foothills," Bob said, looking toward the west.

"There's nothing up there but the caves we're heading for," Linda said thoughtfully.

"Maybe they're prospectors," Kathy said, "checking out those old gold mines."

"Well, they won't find anything," Bob said. "What little ore those mines had was taken out years ago."

"Oil," Larry said, snapping his fingers. "I'll bet you they're looking for oil. Did you see all that gear in the back of the pickup?"

"It looked more like surveying equipment. Anyway, why look for oil on somebody else's land?"

"Well, if they come back here again, they'd better have explanations," Bob said. "Or they'll meet Bronco—and the sheriff."

"Bronco's got other things on his mind," Linda said. As the four of them rode along toward their picnic ground, she told them what she had overheard at the ranch. Both Bob and Kathy listened intently.

"Oh, old Danner is a pain." Larry grinned. "Maybe

it runs in his family. How else can you explain his grandson, Eric?" Everyone laughed.

Kathy's face was quickly concerned again. "They can't really take the ranch away from you, can they? I mean, your family has had it forever."

"Of course they can't," Bob said. "Doña and Bronco will straighten it out." But he looked worried.

"Let's talk about it over lunch," Larry said. "Come on." He kicked Snowbird and galloped ahead of the group.

Amber wanted to run with Snowbird, but Linda held her down to a walk. Larry and the Appaloosa were already looking small in the distance. She watched them veer off to the right and disappear. She wondered why Larry had done that, but you never knew what Larry was up to.

"After we eat," she said, "maybe we should go back to the ranch and ask Mac about that deed. He knows almost as much about the ranch as Doña."

"Good idea," Bob said. "I want to tell him about those guys in the pickup."

"Hey, where's Larry?" Linda let Amber speed up along Larry's trail.

They crossed a dry streambed and turned with the

trail as it led west and slightly north toward the foothills where the old caves were. Larry ought to be in sight by now, Linda thought, but there's no sign of him.

They rode into a field of tall, brown, dried grass. The only sound was the *swoosh* of the grass as the horses passed through it.

Linda looked ahead, but saw only a bird, flying over a grove of trees. She let Amber break into a trot, pulling farther ahead of Bob and Kathy.

Linda and Amber were halfway across the field when the brush in front of them seemed to explode.

A large flock of birds burst into the air together. *Clack-clack-clack!* The racket of their wings was deafening.

Amber whinnied in surprise and leaped sideways. Caught off guard, Linda fell forward onto the saddle horn. Before she could regain her balance, Amber reared up.

Then Linda was flying, too—out of the saddle and toward the hard, sunbaked ground!

3 ✦✦✦✦

Linda opened her eyes and saw Bob's anxious face looking down at her.

"Are you all right?" he said.

"Don't move her," Kathy said. "She might have broken something."

Larry, still on his horse, looked scared. "It was just a joke. I saw those birds and snuck around to charge up and scare them. It was just to surprise you. I never meant to spook the horses. Are you okay?"

"I'm fine—no thanks to you, Larry." Linda carefully moved her arms and legs to make sure nothing was broken. "I just got the wind knocked out of me." She raised herself up on one elbow. "How's Amber?"

"Figures you're more worried about her than about

yourself!" Bob shook his head. "A good trail horse wouldn't spook like that." He helped her up. "Are you sure you're okay?"

"I'm all right, really. And give me a break." Linda glared at her brother. "Even Rocket would jump if a flock of birds flew into his face."

"I just didn't realize you were so close," Larry said. "I'm sorry, Linda."

"Forget it, this time." Linda grinned at him. "I'm okay. Amber's the one who's upset. Poor girl. You scared her." She stroked Amber's soft nose.

Snowbird edged over toward Amber and tried to bite her on the neck. Larry jerked his reins. "Cut it out, Snowbird. We're in enough trouble." He wheeled the horse away from the others.

"Let's go." Linda gathered her reins and climbed into the saddle, moving stiffly.

Bob and Kathy remounted. "Hold Amber in," Bob said to Linda. "I don't want you breaking your neck."

"I can ride as well as you can, and you know it." Linda could feel herself getting annoyed. "And Amber is the best horse I've ever ridden."

Bob shook his head and rode off to catch up with Larry. Linda glared after him.

"Boys think they're so smart," she said.

"I think he was scared you were hurt. Sometimes they sound bossy like that—but they're just worried." Kathy had three older brothers, and she considered herself an authority.

"I wish Larry would worry a little—instead of pulling stupid tricks." Linda brushed some dirt from her knees. "Well, nobody got hurt, so let's get going."

When they caught up with Bob and Larry, the boys had found a shady spot and gotten off their horses. And they were already hard at work on the sandwiches Bob had brought. Linda and Kathy unpacked their saddlebags. Kathy handed out soft drinks.

"Too bad you guys didn't wait. We brought the best food!" Kathy said, tearing open a big package of corn chips.

Linda grinned as she peeled an orange. She popped a section into her mouth and bit down. "Mmm, that tastes good. I was thirsty."

While they were eating, Linda's thoughts went back to the conversation she had overheard that morning. Turning to her brother, she asked, "Why do you think Don Carlos never refiled that deed?"

"I don't know. But then, Don Carlos wasn't just an everyday rancher." He turned to Larry and Kathy.

"When we were kids, Doña used to tell us stories about him, instead of fairy tales."

"Like what?" Kathy asked.

"My favorite was always the snake story." Bob laughed. "I used to drive Doña crazy, asking her to tell that one.

"Once, when his kids were little, Don Carlos saw a rattlesnake creeping up on one of them. He reached out and grabbed the rattler with his bare hands. Then he threw it across the yard, picked up the baby, and walked into the house as if nothing had happened."

Larry stared. "That's a little hard to believe," he said.

"Well, I know *my* favorite story about him is true," Linda said. "Don Carlos went after a wild black stallion who used to kick down people's fences and set their horses loose. Everyone said that no one could catch him, much less ride him.

"Don Carlos spent two years chasing that horse through these hills, but he caught him—and trained him. He named the stallion Sombra—Shadow. He's the black horse in Don Carlos's portrait in the house."

Kathy turned to Linda. "Wow, that's something.

Don Carlos sounds like a character in a book—not the kind of guy you'd find in your backyard."

Bob smiled. "Well, that's where he used to sleep. Even after he built the ranch house, he bedded down outdoors. He said counting the stars put him to sleep."

"I guess he just had his own way of doing things," Linda said. "What if that's the reason he never refiled his deed? Since the original records were destroyed in a fire, maybe he didn't trust the courthouse anymore and didn't even want to send his deed there to be filed?"

"It's probably here on the ranch," Bob offered. "Somewhere he thought was safe, a place that couldn't burn down."

"Let's go find it," Larry said, jumping up and heading for Snowbird.

"And just where are you going to look?" Kathy laughed. "Rancho del Sol is huge. It could be almost anywhere."

Linda considered their choices. "Why not ask Mac? Maybe he'll have an idea."

"All right, let's do it!" Bob agreed. "Let's clean up and get going."

Quickly they packed up the remains of the picnic and unhitched the horses. Bob led off at top speed with Larry right behind him. Linda watched for a moment.

"He's such a good rider," Kathy said.

Linda smiled. Though Kathy would never admit it, Linda suspected she had a crush on Bob. The girls started off at an easy pace. Linda was aching to let Amber run, but she didn't want to leave Kathy behind. She could feel the horse's muscles tighten, and she knew that Amber, too, longed to take off.

Kathy raised her eyebrows as she watched Amber prance. "Oh, go ahead. I'll catch up." She grinned. "Sometime. Patches is a good horse, but he's not in Amber's class."

Linda grinned back and gave Amber a squeeze with her legs. The mare took off with such a burst of speed that Linda was thrown off balance for a moment. Then she pressed her heels down, leaned forward in the saddle, and let Amber have her head.

Amber flew across the fields. In no time at all they caught up with Bob and Larry, but Linda didn't slow down. She heard Bob's shout as she passed them and then the pounding of hooves as the boys tried to catch her. It was a good distance back to the stable, but if Amber could do it, Linda was going to beat the boys.

As they raced on, time seemed to stand still. Nothing was real except the sound of hooves and the wind whistling past Linda's head. They came closer to the stable, and Linda caught a glimpse of Rocket coming up on her left. She leaned even farther forward, like a jockey, as far as the saddle horn would let her. She urged the horse on with her legs and her voice. "Go, Amber! Go!"

Amber's mane streamed backward into Linda's face, and the wind whipped her own dark hair. Out of the corner of her eye she could see Rocket gaining on her. Bob's face was set in determination.

They came to a dry gulch, and both horses jumped it without slowing down. Now they were running neck and neck. Rocket's coat was lathered with sweat, but Amber seemed to stay cool.

The low red-tile roof of the ranch house was in sight now, and the taller roofs of the stable and the cow barn. Rocket began to crowd Amber a little. Once he jerked his head toward her as if to nip her. Amber lengthened her stride. Moments later, Rocket and Bob were half a length behind.

A stone fence came up in front of them now. Linda

could feel Amber's muscles tensing for another leap.
She rose up out of the saddle. That's when she saw a
glint of water.

She'd forgotten about the stream beyond the fence
—and now there was no way to warn—or stop—
Amber!

4 ✦✦✦✦

Linda stood in the stirrups and gave Amber her head, praying that the mare would take off as strongly as possible.

Together, they sprang into the air. The fence flashed below them. Linda held her breath as they kept going. Would they make it?

She glanced down to see water . . . then dirt. Amber landed heavily, jolting Linda forward on her saddle. The horse's rear legs scrambled at the edge of the stream, then she pulled herself forward. She was galloping away by the time Bob and Rocket cleared the fence.

Linda didn't slow down until they'd almost reached the road that led to the stable. Then gradually she collected Amber into a slow lope, and then a smooth sitting trot. Amber responded at once to Linda's signals.

Mac and one of the hands stood in the stable yard watching them. Bob and Rocket were a couple of lengths behind Amber. Larry and Snowbird were just behind Rocket. The cowhand waved and went back to his work. Mac watched with his hands on his hips as the boys brought their horses to a flashy stop, half rearing.

Bob was laughing. "You beat me!" he said to Linda.

Larry fanned his face with his hat, staring at Amber. "That is a horse and a half," he said.

Mac laughed. "That doesn't come as any surprise to Linda."

Bob dismounted and came over to stroke Amber's shoulder. "I take everything back. You're an amazing horse!"

Linda smiled and managed not to say, "I told you so." She and the boys unsaddled their horses and began walking them around the yard to cool them off. In the distance, Kathy and Patches were just coming into sight, moving at a fast trot.

Snowbird kicked out at Rocket as the horses passed each other.

"I'll walk him around in back of the barn for a minute," Larry said. "He's in a bad mood." He grinned at Linda. "A rotten loser. Unlike Bob and me, of course, who are always gentlemen."

Linda laughed as Larry walked away with the Appaloosa. "Larry's a good sport." She glanced at her brother. "So are you."

Bob laughed, too. "Why? Because I didn't kick at you?"

Mac started to walk away toward the cow barn.

"Mac," Bob said, "have you got a minute?"

Mac came back. "What's up?"

"If you have time, we want to talk to you."

Mac tipped his hat back on his head. "I never *have* time," he said with a grin. "But I can *make* time." That was something he used to say to them when they were little and wanted him to give them a riding lesson or help with a new pet calf. "What's on your mind?"

Linda told him what she had overheard. Mac listened carefully, frowning.

"No wonder Bronco and Doña tore out of here like

that. They must have been heading straight to their lawyers."

"There's got to be some mistake." Linda looked pleadingly at Mac. "Hasn't there?"

"I've heard that story about the courthouse burning down," Mac said. "Never thought a whole lot about it. I guess we all figured that Don Carlos refiled the deed." He scratched his thick, curly hair. "Let me think a few minutes."

He glanced at his watch. "Got a couple of things to do right now. Why don't you kids cool down your horses and then come on into my office—say, fifteen minutes? Luisa brought me out a big pitcher of lemonade. I'll share it with you."

"I should probably go home," Kathy said.

From her friend's face Linda knew Kathy was dying to stay but was trying to be polite.

"Come on, hang around. If we go off looking for this deed, we'll want your help."

Kathy grinned. "Thanks."

Larry came back, having left Snowbird in the corral behind the barn. "Who belongs to that little sorrel?"

"What little sorrel?" Bob said. But just then, a commotion caught his attention. "That Nacho is pestering the bay mare again." Nacho was a Shetland pony with a knack for mischief. Bob ran to separate them and calm the jittery bay.

"Mac's going to talk with us about the lost deed," Linda broke in. "Want to stay?"

"You bet," Larry said. "I wouldn't miss it. If anybody knows any clues, it'll be Mac. He's a walking local history book."

"I just hope he knows the answer this time." Linda led Amber into the cool stable and put her in her stall. Amber nuzzled against her, breaking Linda's worried mood. "Take it easy, little horse." She laughed. "You've had a busy day." She patted Amber's neck.

The palomino tossed her head, her dark eyes sparkling. Linda carefully untacked her, lifting off the saddle and bridle. She slowly curried where the saddle had been and smoothed the hair down with a body brush. Both horse and rider enjoyed the time they spent together, and it was nice to steal a few quiet moments after their breakneck ride back to the stable.

Linda could hardly wait to tell Bronco and Doña how well Amber had done on the trail. Smoothing out the long snowy mane and forelock, Linda murmured, "I'll see you after dinner."

Stepping out of the stall, Linda put the brushes

back in the tack room, next to Mac's office. The stable was a big one, with horse stalls along both the east and west sides.

Around three sides, above the stalls and the office, was the hayloft, reached by one ladder at the north end, and another built into the wall at the back. Just behind the stable there was a small corral where Mac sometimes kept troublesome or sick horses.

Linda stood for a moment in the dim light, taking a deep breath of the pleasant, familiar smell of hay. Most of the horses were either out on the range or in the corral. An old brood mare drowsed sleepily in the stall next to Amber's. Some bantam hens pecked at seeds on the dirt floor.

New wings had been added to the house over the years, but the stable was much as it had been when Don Carlos built it. It was very large, so Linda figured Don Carlos must have been sure from the start that he was going to have a successful ranch.

She thought of the oil painting of him that hung in the dining room. It was not a great portrait. Probably, it was done by one of the many wandering painters who roamed the countryside in those days, "painting for their supper."

But Don Carlos's character came through. His

long, outthrust jaw looked a little like Doña's when she was angry. He had a rugged face, with a long mustache and a neatly trimmed beard. Leaning against his black stallion, Shadow, he had a velvet cape tossed casually over his shoulders. He held his head tilted slightly backward, staring at the viewer with the large dark eyes that both Doña and Linda had inherited. And he held a short riding whip in his hands.

If I had been Don Carlos, what would I have done with that deed? Linda wondered.

As she walked toward Mac's office she thought she heard a sound in the hayloft. She stopped and listened, but all she heard was the voices of a couple of ranch hands working outside. She couldn't see anything in the loft. Nothing moved. Maybe it was one of the barn cats looking for a mouse—or a mouse looking for a hiding place.

"It's a risky life, mice," she said aloud.

"Who are you talking to?" Kathy stuck her head in the wide, open doors.

"The mice," Linda said, laughing.

They went into Mac's office and found the boys already there, drinking lemonade from paper cups. Mac's office looked as if nothing had been changed for a hundred years. He sat on a swivel chair that seemed ready to fall apart, in front of a huge rolltop desk with a lot of small drawers. In a big wooden file cabinet next to the desk he kept careful records of ranch business.

When the girls had settled down—Kathy on a broken leather sofa, Linda on a milking stool—Mac linked his hands behind his head and said, "What I figure is this. Don Carlos was nobody's fool. He'd keep the deed in a safe place. And then . . . well, as I recall, he died a year or so after that fire."

"Maybe he just hadn't got around to refiling the deed," Bob said.

"Then what happened to it?" Kathy asked.

Mac waved toward his file cabinet. "The records in there go back to those days, but there's no deed."

"Are you sure, Mac?" Linda said anxiously. "I mean you never really looked for the deed before, did you?"

"That's right. But back about a year ago the priest at the old Mission church who's in charge of archives got permission from Doña to photograph our early records."

"What for?" Larry said.

"History. There aren't many of these old ranches left. So Brother Joseph and I went through all that stuff—and there was no deed."

"It could have disappeared years ago," Bob said.

"What if Don Carlos hid it somewhere?" Linda said. "For safekeeping."

Mac nodded. "It's possible."

Linda felt her heart beginning to speed up. That deed had to be somewhere. Maybe she and Bob and their friends would find it.

Mac stood up. "Well, amigos, I got cattle calling me. There's work to do."

"One more thing, Mac," Bob said. "Do you have anyone surveying on the ranch?"

"There's no reason to—we all know the ranch's borders," Mac answered. "Why do you ask?"

Bob told him about the two men in the pickup truck.

"I got the license-plate number," Linda added.

"Write it down for me. I'll check it out," Mac said.

He stretched and touched his fingertips to the ceiling. "And I'd say the best place for you to look for that deed is up in the attic, at the house."

"That's a great idea," Linda said. "The attic is full

of all kinds of stuff from years and years back." She jumped up, almost knocking over the milking stool she had been perched on. "Let's start right now."

"I have to get home," Kathy said, "but I can come over tomorrow."

"There's so much stuff up there, it will take forever," Linda said.

"I'll help, too," Larry said. "First thing in the morning. And I'll bring some fruit. Searching attics is dusty work."

He started toward the back doors of the stable to get Snowbird.

"What's that?" Linda stared up at the hayloft. "I heard a noise."

They stood listening. And heard only the sound of Amber pushing at her water pail.

"Probably mice," Bob said.

But as he spoke, a clump of hay fell from the loft. One wisp landed on his shoulder.

Linda started for the nearest ladder. Before she could reach it, there was a scampering sound above her.

"That's not mice," she said. "Or cats, either. Somebody's up there!"

Linda scrambled up the ladder and charged into the dark shadows of the hayloft. She saw a crouched figure dive toward the other end of the loft.

"Quick!" she shouted. "Block the other ladder!"

Larry, who had leaped onto the ladder behind Linda, followed her into the loft. Bob ran across the stable to the ladder at the other end, but he was too late. The intruder reached the bottom of the ladder before Bob was halfway there.

As Linda came down the other ladder, she saw the intruder race out the stable door. He jumped onto a sorrel mare and tore off, bent so low over the horse's neck that she couldn't see his face.

"Did you see who it was, Linda?" Bob asked.

"All I saw was a shirt and a pair of jeans," she said. "It looked like a kid, but I didn't see his face."

"Remember I asked you who that sorrel belonged to?" Larry said.

"Yeah, but it went right out of my mind when Nacho started acting up," Bob said. "You know kids sometimes sneak in here to see the horses. We probably scared him. That's why he ran away."

"Who do we know that rides a sorrel?" Kathy asked.

Bob shook his head. "Nobody comes to mind."

"Well, we can start checking around—but not now," said Kathy, glancing at her watch. "I've got to be heading home."

"Me, too," Larry said. "Stay tuned, folks. More thrilling developments tomorrow."

When they had gone, Bob said, "Whoever was in the loft could have heard us talking in Mac's office."

"Maybe so, but it wouldn't mean anything to him, anyway. So it's no big deal if he did," Linda said.

"I guess so." They walked toward the house. Automatically Bob chinned himself on a branch of the huge old valley oak that grew near the back door.

When Linda was little, she used to imagine that the tree, with its curving branches and its cracked leathery bark, was an enormous alligator.

"You're getting too tall to chin yourself on the old alligator," she said. Bob had grown several inches in the last year. He would soon be as tall as Bronco.

Stretching up toward the top of the tree, Bob pointed to the roof of the house. "When do you want to look up there?" he asked.

"How about tonight, after dinner?" Linda suggested.

"Sounds good to me," Bob replied.

When the family gathered for dinner that evening, Bob and Linda found their grandparents unusually quiet.

Doña broke the silence. "I'm afraid that Mr. Danner gave us some bad news today. We thought you two should know about it."

Linda and Bob exchanged glances. "We already know." Linda explained. "I heard you talking with Mr. Danner. I didn't mean to eavesdrop . . ."

"Well, we were all pretty angry—I wouldn't be

surprised if everyone on the ranch heard us." Doña sighed heavily.

It almost broke Linda's heart to see the worried looks on her grandparents' faces. "Could the deed be somewhere on the ranch?" she asked.

"Maybe Don Carlos didn't trust the courthouse, so he left it here." Bob turned to his grandmother. "Did you ever hear anything about Don Carlos having hiding places?"

"Not really." Doña shook her head. "And knowing Don Carlos, if he had one, it could be just about anywhere on the ranch. I'll have to think about it—Rancho del Sol is just too big to try searching everywhere."

"We wouldn't mind looking," Linda said. "We'd do anything to help."

Bronco looked at her for a long moment. "You kids are not to worry about this mix-up over the deed. We'll take care of it." He added firmly, "This is just some legal technicality. Our lawyers are already working on it."

Linda hoped so. Rancho del Sol was their whole life. She couldn't imagine Doña and Bronco being thrown out of their own home, losing everything. A horrible thought passed through Linda's mind. It would mean she would lose Amber, too. More than ever, she was determined to find that deed and save the ranch.

"Mac thought we should look in the attic," Linda suggested. "Is it okay to do that?"

"Why not?" Bronco smiled. "When are you going to do it?"

"Right after dinner," Linda answered, happy to be doing something to help. "We can bed down the horses after we finish."

"Speaking of horses, how did Amber do today?" Bronco asked, changing the subject. "Any trouble?"

Linda shot a quick glance at Bob. Would he tell Bronco about her fall?

Her brother just shook his head. "Amber has to be one of the fastest horses I've ever seen. On the way back to the ranch, Linda rode her right past Rocket and Snowbird as if they were standing still."

Linda started to grin, but Bob went on. "Of course, she's still not an experienced trail horse—like Rocket."

Bob had set her up, and she was trapped. If she tried to argue, to defend Amber, he'd tell how Amber had acted up. "Oh, of course!" Linda forced herself to say. "But we all know you think Rocket is the world's greatest horse."

Now it was Linda's turn to try and shift the conversation to something else. She turned to her grandfather. "While we were out on the trail, we saw something we wanted to ask you about."

"What's that?" Bronco asked.

"Two men in a pickup truck. It looked like maybe they were surveying, or looking for oil or something."

"We asked them what they were doing," Bob added. "They wouldn't answer, and then they took off in a hurry."

Bronco's face went hard. "Looking for oil, eh? Vultures come flapping in pretty fast."

"And you didn't recognize them?" Doña said.

"Nope. Linda gave Mac the truck's license-plate number, and he's going to try and check it out."

Their grandparents were quiet for a moment, but Linda saw that Doña was holding tightly to Bronco's hand. Her own heart seemed to squeeze for a second.

"Well, if you kids want to invade the attic, you'd better get started." Doña's voice was light, but Linda could see the look she was aiming at Bronco. They wanted to talk—and without Linda and Bob around.

"That's right," Bronco said. "There must be a hundred years of junk up there—it will take you awhile to get through it all."

Linda and Bob got up from the table and headed up the stairs. At the top of the attic staircase, Bob groped until he found the cord for the light. It was just a single bulb hanging from the ceiling, and it left shadows along the walls and in all the corners of the attic.

"I should have brought my flashlight," Bob said. "Ouch." He had hit his head on a beam.

Linda's foot brushed something that gave off a loud twang. "Hey, it's an old guitar."

"Is it any good?"

Linda picked it up and shook her head. "I don't think so. The neck's cracked. Why would anyone want to save this junk?" she asked, holding out a straw hat with a hole in the top. "Why not just throw it away?"

"Who knows?" Bob gave her a sly grin. "By the way, you owe me one for not telling Bronco about Amber spooking."

"You mean that trick you pulled at the table? I don't think so, Bob. And I don't think Bronco would have liked hearing about Larry's trick out on the ride, either. It wasn't just Amber you were keeping out of trouble."

Bob looked at her for a second. "Um, yeah . . . look, I'm going to go down and get my flashlight. We won't find anything if we can't see it."

He retreated quickly, and Linda began poking around in the attic. Even though her eyes had adjusted to the darkness, she still found herself tripping over boxes. Finally, she went back to the stairs to wait for Bob and his flashlight.

The light from downstairs spilled up around the top of the staircase, cutting the dark to a murky dimness. Linda saw an old armchair facing the wall. She sat in it, sneezed at the dust—and then saw a pair of eyes glaring at her from the wall.

With a yell, Linda jumped back, nearly overturning the chair. Bob appeared, flashing a beam of light onto the old oil painting in front of her. He laughed. "What did you think it was, a ghost?"

Linda let out her breath. "I thought it was . . . I don't know. Maybe a spy, like that person in the stable."

"Nope. That's Don Carlos's oldest son, Juan. I remember Doña having it moved up here. She said he looked too fierce to be downstairs with civilized people."

"I forgot all about him," Linda said. She felt like an idiot. "Let's keep looking."

With the help of the light, they began searching the attic. Linda found a small leather chest and opened the lid. She picked up a bundle of old letters tied together with a blue ribbon. "Look, letters from Thomas J. Mallory . . ."

"That's Bronco."

". . . to Rosalinda Perez."

"Doña. Must be their old love letters."

"How romantic! They must be from before they were married." Linda thought of Bronco and Doña's wedding portrait downstairs in the living room. In the picture they looked so young and so happy. And they'd looked so tired and worried at supper. Sighing, Linda put the letters back in the leather chest and placed it on top of a sealed carton.

Bob interrupted her thoughts. "Doña said there's a trunk of Don Carlos's things up here. Let's see if we can find it."

Together they moved across the attic floor. In a far corner, they spotted a large trunk covered with tooled leather. The initials *C. P.* had been embossed on the cover.

"C. P.!" Linda exclaimed. "Don Carlos Perez!"

"Let's see what's inside," Bob said, opening the latch and lifting up the cover. He reached into the trunk and dangled a pair of tarnished silver spurs. "Wow, I bet these are what he used when he'd go off riding on Shadow." Bob's eyes gleamed. "Do you think Doña would let me have these? Polished up, they'd be great!"

Linda shook her head. "Forget about the spurs, we're looking for the deed!" She pushed the flashlight into his hands. "You hold this. I'll check out the trunk." She pulled out some clothing and a pair of scuffed boots. Then came a studded bridle. Linda held it up to admire for a second, then put it firmly aside. Then, over in a corner . . . "Hey, it's a saddlebag—full of papers!"

The saddlebag was jammed with crumbling parchment, as well as some old ledger books and notebooks. Linda was so excited she wanted to dump everything out and rummage through it.

Instead, though, she hooked the bag's strap over her shoulder and carefully removed the contents, one by one. Some of the old papers were so fragile that she barely dared to unfold them. One heavy piece of parchment was thicker than the others, and had a wax seal on the bottom. Linda gasped when she saw what was written on the top. "By order of the governor, state of California . . ."

"I don't believe it." She turned to Bob. "We just found the deed!"

6 ◆◆◆◆

"What? Are you kidding?" Bob asked. "What does it say?"

"Here, look here!" Linda answered. "It says it's from the governor, and it says some stuff about Don Carlos Perez, and then comes a whole bunch of legal stuff."

"We did it!" Bob hollered. "Let's show Bronco and Doña."

"I can't wait to see the looks on their faces when we hand them this!" Linda said eagerly. "Let's go!"

Using Bob's flashlight to see, they quickly went back to the stairs. They raced down to the main floor of the house. "Doña! Bronco! Where are you?" Linda called.

Doña's voice answered from the living room. "We're in here. What's up? You two sound awfully excited."

Bob and Linda charged into the room. With a huge grin, Linda handed the paper to Doña. "I believe you were looking for this—the deed to the ranch!"

Bronco jumped up from his chair. "You found it? I don't believe it!"

Doña, smiling, started reading the paper. She squinted in concentration as her eyes passed over the words. Then her smile disappeared. She sighed at her grandchildren with disappointment in her eyes.

"I'm sorry, but this isn't the deed," she said gently. "This is just a formal proclamation from the governor thanking Don Carlos for capturing a stagecoach robber—what they call here a 'road agent.'"

Linda felt tears well up in her eyes. "Oh, Doña, are you sure? I was so excited, I didn't read the whole thing."

Bronco came over and put his arm around Linda's shoulders. "Now, honey, it's okay. I told you we would take care of this, and we will. Don't be too disappointed."

"I really thought we had saved the day," Bob said

disgustedly. The silver spurs he was still holding jingled in his hands.

"What else did you find there?" Bronco asked.

"Oh, these. I think they were Don Carlos's spurs. Aren't they beautiful?"

"Why don't you keep them?" Doña said. "After all, he is your great-great-grandfather." She turned to Linda. "Is that Don Carlos's saddlebag?" she asked, pointing to the sac over Linda's arm.

"Yes. I ran down here so fast, I forgot I still had it."

"Well, let's look at it," Doña suggested. "Did you go through everything?"

"No," Linda replied. "When I thought I had found the deed, we came down here. Maybe it's still in there."

They emptied the papers onto the coffee table, and Doña and Bronco carefully unfolded each one. When they had finished, there was still no deed.

Linda leafed through a notebook. "Look, it's an old songbook." She flipped through the pages. "This is strange. This page has our cattle brand marked on it in gold."

She handed the book to her grandfather.

Bronco flipped through the musty pages. "Some

old range songs. Some Spanish songs. And even love songs."

Linda showed him the one with the brand.

"That's interesting," Bronco observed. "I wonder why he did that."

Doña smiled. "Who knows with Don Carlos? He was always busy making a deal, or outfoxing a road agent, or figuring a way to get his cattle to market before anybody else. I'm surprised he found time to write songs as well."

"Don't forget looking for gold in all those caves," Bob said.

"He didn't find any fortune there," Bronco said.

"Maybe not," Doña said with a smile. "But I've got a golden nugget that came from one of those caves."

"Well, I know a golden horse who needs to be bedded down," Linda said. She got up, putting the songbook in the pocket of her denim jacket.

"Wait up," Bob said, following her. "I've got to take care of Rocket."

As they walked to the stable, Bob shook his head. "Don Carlos was a sharp character. I don't believe he just got forgetful and lost his copy of the deed," he said.

"I don't, either."

Linda left her jacket on the little table in the tack room. Then she went to see Amber.

Amber watched with her usual interest as Linda forked clean straw onto the floor of the stall, filled her water bucket, and got her some oats.

"You had a good day, didn't you." Linda combed out Amber's silky mane until it was smooth and shiny. Amber nuzzled Linda's shoulder. "And we showed that nippy old Snowbird, didn't we?"

Bob called from Rocket's stall, "Linda, where's the songbook?"

"In my coat—on the table in the tack room."

A minute later, as she brushed Amber, she heard Bob playing a song on his harmonica. It sounded familiar, but she couldn't think of the name. She wondered if Don Carlos had played those romantic songs to his wife.

Amber turned until her eyes were level with Linda's. Linda patted her neck, then leaned against Amber's shoulder. The horse lifted her right front hoof so Linda could clean it. She finished the other hooves and leaned against Amber's warm side. Bob continued playing Don Carlos's songs.

Linda got a stiff, hard brush to flick the dirt off

Amber's coat and then a body brush to smooth it down. All around her, horses were crunching hay, and occasionally stamping a hoof in their stalls. This was Linda's favorite place on the whole ranch.

Finally, when she could think of no more excuses to linger, she hugged Amber. "See you tomorrow."

Amber took Linda's sleeve in her teeth as if to keep her a little longer. Linda laughed and released it. "Be a good girl."

She went into the tack room and found Bob seated at the table. The notebook was open in front of him as he picked his way through a song. Outside it was getting dark, and she could hear the cicadas making a steady buzz in the air. The gray shadow of a kingbird flew past the door, chasing insects.

"Play the song that has the brand," she said. "What was it called?"

Bob flipped some pages. "'The Golden Secret.' Here it is." He looked over the notes, then played them. "Funny kind of tune."

"I wonder if Don Carlos wrote it himself." Linda started reading the words:

"My Children, where the coyote sings,
Find my Treasure, in the dark and cold.

Where my Shadow roamed, 'neath golden rings,
With my Treasure safe, I need no gold."

She looked at Bob. "That doesn't make sense to
me."

"Love songs don't need to make sense." Bob
turned to a song he knew, and a moment later Linda
was singing "Oh, Susannah."

Mac came and stood in the doorway. He was
showered and shaved and dressed for an evening in
town, wearing his best whipcord pants and a blue
shirt with a string tie. His boots were shiny ones he
saved for dressing up.

When they'd finished, he said, "I heard you song-
birds way down by the bunkhouse. It's enough to
spook the cattle." But he was grinning.

"We found Don Carlos's songbook," Linda said.

"And the deed?"

"Not yet." Linda shook her head in disappointment.

"You're not giving up, are you?" Mac went into his
office and came out carrying a white cowboy hat.

"No," Linda said. "We'll just have to give it more
time." She smiled as she watched Mac put on his hat.
"You look great."

"Must have a new girl," Bob said, winking at Linda.

"No, no." Mac laughed. He tilted the hat slightly over one eye and threw them a wave.

After he had gone, Linda called good night to Amber once more. Then they put out the lights and started for the house. Linda began humming the words of that odd little tune of Don Carlos's: "'. . . Where the coyote sings . . .'" She stopped. The lines kept running in her head.

They came into the kitchen, where Luisa was mixing some Mexican chocolate in milk with a teaspoonful of cinnamon. "A little cocoa to help you go to sleep," she said.

When they had finished and Luisa had headed upstairs to her own little apartment, Linda looked over Don Carlos's songbook one more time. In the back of her mind, something about that odd song with the gold brand was bothering her. She just couldn't put her finger on what it was.

As she and Bob were going upstairs, Linda suddenly said, "Maybe it isn't a love song at all."

"Huh?" Bob looked sleepy.

"'Find my Treasure, in the dark and cold.' That

doesn't sound very romantic. What does he mean by 'Treasure'?"

Bob shrugged. "His girlfriend?"

"Come on, Bob. This is important." She poked him. "Don't go to sleep on me."

He yawned at her. "All right, what are you getting at?"

"What was the greatest treasure he had?" As they reached Bob's door she grabbed him to make him wait. "I'll tell you—the ranch. That's what his treasure was."

"Linda, get to the point."

"I'm *at* the point. I've got it!"

"Got what?"

"I know where Don Carlos hid the deed!"

7 ♦♦♦♦

"What!" Bob's eyes flew open. "What do you mean, you know where the deed is? Don't do this to me twice in one night."

"No, this is different. I know the general area. At least I think I do." In the face of Bob's questions, she didn't feel quite so sure. "The clue is in that song, 'The Golden Secret.'"

"Clue?" He went into his room, switching on the light, and turned as she followed him. "What are you talking about? This had better be good."

"Well, if Rancho del Sol was Don Carlos's greatest treasure, and if the song is talking about the deed to the ranch—"

Bob interrupted. "People don't write songs about ranches and deeds." He yawned.

"He might, if he was trying to hide the deed. Maybe he thought somebody burned down the court-house on purpose. Anyway, if he means Rancho del Sol when he says 'my Treasure,' then he might be talking about where he hid the deed."

She hummed the tune for a moment. "He seems to be talking about a lot of places. 'Where the coyote sings.' And again, 'Where my Shadow roamed.' I just can't get it to make sense."

"*None* of it makes any sense. Go to bed and we'll talk it over in the morning."

But Linda wouldn't budge. "Bob! We're being dense. *Where* did his Shadow roam?"

Bob yawned again. "Wherever the sun happened to be shining. I don't know. Can't it wait for morning?" He sat on the bed and began to take off his boots.

"Okay, if you're not interested." She started for the door.

Bob looked up, his boot half off. "Wait a second. You may as well finish what you started. What's so important about his shadow?"

"What if Shadow is a name?" Linda asked. "Don Carlos called his horse Sombra—Shadow. And he chased that horse all over the hills on the west end of the ranch."

Bob shook his head. "Those hills still give us a lot of ground to cover—on a guess."

"But there's more. The song says the treasure is 'in the dark and cold,' and mentions ''neath golden rings.' Where do you think that might be?"

"I can't think of anyplace like that in the whole ranch." Bob stared at her. "Can you?"

Linda stepped into the hall. "How about an old gold mine?" She tossed the words at him without looking back.

Bob jumped up, one boot half off, and limped after her. "I never thought of that," he said softly. "But there are a lot of those old caves where they looked for gold."

"I know. But at least we'll have narrowed down where we ought to be searching."

Bob looked at her. "You really think Don Carlos would hide the deed to his ranch in an abandoned gold mine?"

"Maybe it wasn't abandoned then. Anyway, that was the old days. Banks got robbed all the time. This might have been the safest place he could think of."

"It's worth a look, I guess. But maybe we'd better tell Doña and Bronco. Let them handle it."

"Let's look first. We don't want to get anyone's hopes up." Linda didn't say so, but she didn't want to give up the excitement of looking for the deed herself, either.

"Well, okay."

"Larry said he'd be here first thing in the morning. I'll call Kathy and tell her."

The next day Linda woke at the crack of dawn. She dressed, made some breakfast, and put together enough lunch for the four of them. Then she headed for the stable.

"'Morning, Linda," one of the ranch hands called out. "You're up early."

"I couldn't sleep."

"Me, I could sleep till noon." He unlatched Amber's stall door. "I hear this little mare's got some speed in her."

"Yesterday she outran Rocket," Linda said proudly.

The ranch hand grinned and stood out of Linda's way as she led Amber from the stall. "The word is out," she whispered in her horse's ear. "They've heard about how fast you are. You're getting famous." She led Amber over to the watering trough.

It was the time of day Linda liked best. The air was cool, and half a dozen doves sat on the telephone wires, making their soft moaning sound.

"I hope I'm right about the deed," she said aloud to herself. "If I'm not, my name is going to be mud, dragging everyone into those stuffy caves. Kathy's going to hate it, and Bob will never let me forget it if I'm wrong again." Amber nudged Linda with her nose, her eyes shining with excitement.

Linda laughed. "Well, I'm glad somebody likes my ideas."

"I've always wanted an excuse to explore those caves," Larry said, when the four friends were finally riding out across the ranch. He and Kathy were as excited about Linda's idea as she was.

"Let's do it right, though," Bob said. "We don't want them to cave in on us."

"Cave in?" Suddenly Kathy looked scared. Linda could tell that the idea of going inside those caves made her nervous.

"Don't worry. I brought extra rope." Bob pointed to the lengths of rope hanging from his saddle horn. "We'll rope ourselves together."

Larry saw the look on Kathy's face and grinned. "That's so if we get buried alive, at least we'll all be together. It's cozier that way."

"Larry!" Linda rode closer to Kathy. "He's kidding."

"Caves do fall in, sometimes," Kathy said.

"Yup. That's the hole story. Get it? H-O-L-E?" Larry kicked Snowbird's sides and galloped off, laughing. Bob followed.

"Don't mind him," Linda said. But seeing that Kathy still looked worried, she added, "One of us ought to stay outside anyway, to get help—just in case. You can be the one."

"They'll think I'm chicken."

"No, they won't. They'll be so excited about exploring the cave, they won't think of anything else."

Kathy looked relieved.

As they rode along, Linda was thinking that Amber was certainly getting experienced as a trail horse. She leaned forward, enjoying the rhythm of Amber's smooth gait. Suddenly Amber sprang sideways, and Linda almost went tumbling.

"It's just an old log, silly," Linda said. "Take it easy."

"Patches wouldn't spook if the log stood right up and talked to him," Kathy said. "Sometimes I wish he had a little more imagination."

"He's a good horse," Linda said. "Maybe not exciting, but sturdy."

They met the boys by a shallow stream in the foothills near the caves. A small pond green with algae gave off a stagnant smell, but the breeze from the mountains was cool. And the trees that grew along the stream provided shade. Birds called out from the dark green of the trees. It was a perfect picnic spot.

The four riders let their horses drink and splash in the stream before they tied them. When Linda tried to hitch Amber to a pine tree, she pawed the ground and tossed her mane and whinnied.

"Come on, girl, settle down," Linda coaxed, stroking her neck.

"She shouldn't be so edgy," Bob said. He shook his head.

As Linda spread out the food she'd brought, Larry said, "Hey, I was supposed to bring fruit for the attic search, wasn't I?"

Everyone groaned. Larry was famous for forgetting things.

"Well, surprise! I did!"

He passed the fruit. Kathy had brought sandwiches, too, so there was more than enough food. And they managed to eat most of it.

Larry, finishing off his third sandwich, jumped up. "Let's go," he said. "Anybody know exactly where these caves are?"

"We know where some of them are," Bob said. "Once Mac took us exploring and showed us where Don Carlos actually found gold. We'll try that one over by the pine trees first." He pointed to a pile of rocks just beyond some scrub pines.

"I wouldn't mind finding some gold," Larry said.

"I just want to find the deed," Linda said. "We may not find anything at all," she added under her breath.

Bob was busy roping himself to Larry.

"Kathy's going to stay outside," Linda said.

Larry grinned. "That makes me feel a lot safer. You can stand guard, Kathy. If any bad guys ride up, don't tell 'em we're inside. And whatever you do, don't tell 'em about the gold."

Kathy gave him a scornful look. "I don't have to worry about bad guys. I'll just let *you* talk them to death!"

"Come on," Linda said as Bob finished roping her

to Larry. "Let's go." She walked away from the picnic place toward the rocky hillside. Because they were all roped together, Bob and Larry had to follow. Bob carried a pick and shovel. When they got to the cave entrance, he and Larry began chopping away at the stones and twigs that filled the opening to the cave.

A wooden doorway had been built to protect the mouth of the cave, but most of it had rotted away. They would have to crawl in on their hands and knees.

Bob unhooked his flashlight from his belt. "I'll go first. Let's take it slow. We don't want the roof falling in on us. The timbers holding up these caves must be a hundred years old. They could break if you hit them."

Linda held her breath as she crawled into the darkness. For a second, she felt as if the whole weight of the hill were pressing down on her. It was too dark to see anything except the beam from Bob's flashlight ahead of them, and even that seemed faint in the cave. Linda bumped her knee on a half-buried root and said, "Ouch!" Her voice sounded hollow as it echoed off the cave walls.

Larry, just ahead of her, said, "Yuk!"

A moment later she felt cobwebs wrapping around her face, and she knew what he meant. She could almost feel spiders crawling on her.

They moved carefully along the walls, feeling for shelves or pockets where a deed could be hidden. Linda was glad she could hear the boys' heavy breathing as they crawled ahead of her. Even though they were tied together, she had a strange feeling of being all alone.

As they inched forward, Linda began to feel more confident. She had expected the cave to be damp and slimy, filled with mud. Actually it was quite dry, even dusty.

She heard something moving ahead of her, and figured it must be Larry's toe, slipping along the rock. Too late, she realized the sound was closer than that. She put her hand on the ground, groping forward, and touched something dry and slithery. It moved under her palm. A snake!

Linda jerked back her hand and tried to jump to her feet, hitting her head on the roof of the tunnel. "Guys, there are snakes in here."

"Oh, right," said Bob. "I saw one in the beam of my light. It's not a rattler. Not dangerous."

"Well, thanks for telling me. I put my *hand* on

him." She thought of Kathy, outside in the sunshine. She really had the best job. Spiders and snakes —what could be worse?

"Hold it," Bob said. "The path ends."

"Good," Larry said. "I don't think I could go much longer. My knees are killing me."

"There's a room here," Bob said. "About five feet high."

"Then we can turn around," Larry said. "Beats crawling out backward."

"A real room?" Linda said. Maybe the deed was there.

"Come and look. But watch your heads. Don't try to stand up straight or you'll be sorry."

"Ouch," Larry said as he stood up too quickly. "You were right."

It took a lot of squeezing and maneuvering and stepping on each other's feet before they were all crouched together in the tiny room. Bob played the flashlight slowly over the walls.

"Here's something," Linda said. "A shelf dug out of the rock."

"I have one request," Larry said, crunched against the wall. "Don't drop that flashlight."

All three of them felt around the cramped walls.

Linda checked the shelf, and her fingers brushed metal. "Bob, flash the light over here."

The light reflected off an old lantern. Bob laughed. "I guess they didn't have flashlights in the 1880s."

"Not even a gold nugget to take home for a paperweight," Larry said. "Ouch!" He cracked his head again on the overhang. "Look, it's not that I'm not having a great time, but do you think we could get out of here now?"

Bob agreed. "Well, one cave down . . . ," he said as he moved out of the room.

Larry followed, remembering to duck, and they formed a line again, carefully crawling out of the cave. Linda had grabbed the lantern, and she took it out with her.

The way back seemed even longer to Linda than coming in. She was tired and cold and her knees were getting sore.

"Hey—I can see light!" Bob yelled.

Linda lifted her head and blinked. A short distance ahead of them, a pale shaft of light came through the entrance to the cave. They were almost there.

Then they heard Kathy screaming in terror.

"Kathy!" Linda cried out.

The rope jerked as Bob scrambled out of the cave. She heard him say, "Amber! No!"

Larry crawled quickly out of the cave, pulling the line tight. Linda burst through the cave opening at full speed, dropping the lantern. A shower of dirt fell on her from overhead.

She blinked, half-blinded. Then she saw Kathy backed helplessly against a tree. In front of her was Amber, neighing and rearing.

The mare's ears were flat against her head, and her nostrils flared wildly. Kathy shrank back in terror, unable to retreat any farther.

Then Amber reared again, her hooves lashing the air inches from Kathy's face!

8 ◆◆◆◆

"Amber! Stop!" Linda darted forward and grabbed Amber's reins. She gently pulled the trembling mare away from Kathy. With one hand, she yanked at the rope around her stomach until the knot gave way. Then she pulled Amber's head around until she was looking into the mare's dark eyes.

"What happened?" Linda asked gently, stroking Amber's sweating neck. "There, you're all right." She was almost crooning to the horse. "Easy, Amber, easy . . ."

Behind her Linda could hear Kathy crying, and the two boys calming her down. Over her shoulder she asked, "What *did* happen, Kathy?"

"I don't know. That's what's so awful." Kathy blew

her nose. "All of a sudden, Amber was rearing and whinnying."

"Are you okay?" Linda asked her friend.

"Just shaken up," Kathy replied. "I'm glad you all came out when you did."

"Me, too," Bob said grimly. "I don't think Amber's ready for the trail yet. She's still too nervous."

"She is not! Something must have happened."

Gently Linda ran her hands over Amber's legs, looking for a bee sting or a snake bite—something that might have spooked her.

"Did you find anything in the mine?" Kathy asked.

"Just this." Bob shook his head in disgust as he picked up the old lantern.

"And a snake," Larry added.

"That was only one mine," Linda said, still searching for whatever might have scared Amber. "Hey!" She ran a hand over Amber's rump.

"What?" Bob said.

"She's got big bumps on her hide. Something must have bitten her."

When Bob touched one of the marks, Amber skittered sideways. "It's okay," Linda soothed.

Bob looked at the bumps carefully. "Could she have gotten stung by hornets or something?"

"I didn't see any hornets," Kathy said.

"Maybe you were too busy looking out for bad guys," Larry said. Then he smiled. "I'm sorry I teased you before. Having a horse go wild on you is worse than anything that happened inside."

Amber's ears flattened, and she backed up.

"What is it?" But as soon as Linda asked, she heard a rustling in the brush near the cave.

"Somebody's there!" Bob ran toward the bushes.

A boy bolted out of the scrub and scrambled off toward a grove of pines. Larry jumped to his feet, but it was Bob who brought the boy to the ground with a hard tackle.

Linda stayed with Amber, who was trembling again. "Who is it? Can you see?" she said to Kathy.

"I don't believe it. It's Eric Danner," Kathy answered.

Linda frowned. "What's he doing around here?"

They watched Bob and Larry drag the struggling boy into the open. As they came back to the clearing, they jerked him to his feet. He tried to slip out of their hold, but he couldn't.

"Let go!" Eric was scrawny, with red hair cut so close that he almost looked scalped. He wore jeans and a T-shirt, and expensive tooled-leather boots. "Get your hands off me."

"What are you doing here?" Bob demanded. "Did you scare that horse?"

"She sure did rear!" A mean little grin narrowed Eric's mouth. "But I didn't do a thing," he added quickly. "She just started acting up. Guess she's too spooky to be any good."

"You little worm." Larry looked at Amber, who was still trying to back away from Eric. "What did you do?"

"Nothing."

"Oh yeah?" Kathy jumped behind Eric and pulled a slingshot from his rear pocket. "I bet you shot at Amber with this."

Eric tried again to break away, twisting from side to side. That just made Bob and Larry hold him tighter. "I did not," Eric said. "I didn't do anything."

"You're right, Kathy. He shot rocks at her," Linda said. "That's what made these big welts. Poor Amber —no wonder she was scared."

Eric was staring at the toes of his boots. "It was just a joke. I didn't think it would make her go wild like that," he said. His voice was sullen and so low it was hard to hear him.

77

"Suppose Amber had hurt Kathy?" Larry said angrily. "That would have been no joke!"

"What are you doing here, anyway?" Linda said. "This is a long way from town."

"What's it to you?" Eric glared at them.

"It's our ranch, that's what," Bob shot back.

"Not for long, it's not. My grandfather's going to get it. Nobody beats Silas Danner. He's got tricks he hasn't even used yet."

Bob and Linda stared at each other in shock. "What are you talking about?" Linda cried.

"I've heard my grandfather talking. He's going to take it from you. And I heard you in the stable. You can't even find a deed for your ranch."

"You little snoop. That was you in the hayloft!" Larry said. "I ought to—"

"Go ahead and try"—Eric sneered—"and my grandfather will get you. My family owns this town. My grandfather owns the bank. My father is the vice-president. We've got the biggest house and best swimming pool around. And we're going to own this ranch."

"I wouldn't count on that. We're not giving it up." Bob looked at Linda. "Do we let him go?"

Linda led Amber over. The mare's nostrils flared,

and she flattened her ears as she came closer to Eric. "Did somebody send you out here to spy on us?" Linda said.

"Huh?" Eric stared at her.

"Your grandfather isn't after this ranch for himself," Linda pressed. Bob leaned forward to see Eric's face when he answered.

"That's what you think." Taking advantage of Bob's relaxed hold, Eric jerked free.

Bob grabbed for him, but Eric was too fast. He scooted into the bushes. A moment later a sorrel horse came crashing out with Eric on his back. Galloping off, he called over his shoulder, "So long—and say good-bye to your ranch!"

"I'm going after that little weasel!" Larry leaped onto Snowbird.

"So it's Danner who's after the ranch," Linda said. "He wants it for himself."

"Wait till Doña hears that!" Bob said.

"And now we know who rides a sorrel," Kathy added.

Bob watched Larry galloping after Eric. "He's crazy to go chasing after him."

"Larry is always chasing something," Kathy said, "whether it makes sense or not."

Linda continued to stroke Amber. The mare had quieted down, but she was still tense.

So was Kathy. Her face was grim as they mounted up. "Eric Danner is one of those kids who goes out of his way to make people hate him."

"It would be easy to hate him if his family got their hands on this ranch," Bob said. He gazed across the fields, as if he had never really looked at them before.

But Linda looked at Amber. If they lost the ranch, they'd lose their horses, and that was something Linda just couldn't bear. She wouldn't let the Danners take the ranch—and Amber—away.

Amber crowded into Rocket, getting a frown from Bob. "Watch your horse, Linda."

Blushing, Linda let Kathy and Bob ride off ahead. She turned Amber in a tight circle and then pulled her up. "I know you're still upset, but you've got to behave. Understand?"

Amber pawed the ground impatiently, but Linda held her where she was. The horse turned, giving Linda an annoyed look. Then Amber lowered her head, shaking it so that her silvery forelock fell forward over her face.

Kathy and Bob couldn't be far ahead, but they were out of sight, in a dip of the land. Linda walked Amber. She was in no mood to catch up with the others. She wanted time to think.

Just because the deed wasn't in the mine they'd explored didn't mean it wasn't in any of them. They should look . . .

Linda was jogged out of her thoughts as Amber sidestepped off the trail. "Quit it, Amber!" she said.

When she tried to get back on the trail, Amber resisted. "What's your problem?" Then Linda saw the hoofprints angling off toward the mesa. Two horses. Eric must have chosen the quickest way home, even though it was a lot rougher, and Larry had followed.

"Sorry, Amber," Linda said. "You saw what we all should have been looking for." She stood up in her stirrups, searching for any sign of Eric or Larry. "Snowbird's not exactly hard to pick out, so why can't I see him?"

Suddenly Amber jumped again, sending Linda thumping back into the saddle. "What now? Eric's nowhere near here!"

Amber's eyes were wide. She puffed and snorted, prancing nervously. Linda couldn't understand what was going on. Then she heard a distant rumbling and understood. "Earthquake!" Quickly she slipped out of the saddle and led Amber over to smooth ground. "Easy, Amber."

The earth trembled again, more violently. Amber skittered nervously, pawing at the ground. Linda held the reins slack at the ends, giving the horse plenty of room to trot back and forth until she calmed down.

"Come on." Linda patted Amber's side. "Take it easy. I won't let anything happen to you. How about some more sugar?" She found a lump in her pocket, but Amber was too nervous to eat it.

Linda gently ran her hand up the reins toward Amber's head. She walked the mare up and down, one hand on her neck. "See? It's just a little jiggle or two, then it's over."

After several minutes passed without any more tremors, Linda said, "That's it. Let's catch up with the others. Quakes make Rocket nervous." Linda mounted Amber and urged her into a slow, collected trot.

She met Kathy and Bob riding back to check on her. "I thought Amber would be halfway to Honolulu by now," Bob said with a grin.

"She did fine. How about Rocket?"

Bob's grin became a bit sheepish.

"If Bob weren't such a good rider, he'd have been sitting on the ground, right behind Rocket's tail," Kathy said.

Linda smiled. "Maybe you should watch *your* horse, Bob." She and Kathy grinned at each other.

"What did Patches do?" Linda asked Kathy.

"Are you kidding? He wrinkled his skin the way he does when the flies bother him. That was it." Kathy scratched between Patches' ears. "Nothing upsets this horse."

"Well, Amber is still upset about something."

The mare began pulling off the trail again, toward the mesa. Linda had to jerk on the reins to get her back.

"Show her who's boss," Bob said. "Don't give in to her."

"Oh, stop telling me how to ride!" Linda pulled on her reins again. "Just go along. We'll catch up."

"You don't have to get mad," Bob said.

Amber turned her head toward the mesa and whinnied. Her ears were pricked sharply forward as if she were listening. She whinnied again and looked at Linda impatiently. Then she jumped across the shallow ditch beside the trail.

Faintly, Linda heard another horse neighing. It came from the distance, toward the mesa. "Bob! Did you hear that? Somebody's in trouble!" She let Amber have her head.

The mare stretched into a gallop. Linda could hear Rocket and Patches cantering up behind her. Amber charged ahead at full speed. Linda hoped they wouldn't stumble into a rabbit hole. She just held on tight and let the mare fly.

Without slowing down, Amber darted around a pile of rocks, then ran so close to a clump of stunted pines that Linda instinctively ducked. But Amber knew what she was doing.

The ground rose gradually as they approached the cliffs of the mesa. With all the loose rock lying on the ground, Amber began to slow down.

Linda pushed her hair out of her face to see better. They were coming straight at the mesa, about in the middle of it. Larry had headed this way, but she didn't see him or Snowbird anywhere.

Now they were in the shadows of the mesa. Bushes grew thickly at the base, and there were big boulders. Amber stepped around a large rock, making her way to the foot of the hill. Linda didn't try to guide her.

Bob called out. "What's up?"

"I don't know." She patted Amber's neck, and the hide rippled. Like goose bumps, Linda thought. She wondered if Eric Danner had been crazy enough to ride up over the mesa. He could break his neck, riding up there. And Larry should have had sense enough not to follow. This was rough, dangerous terrain. Horses should be walked here, not ridden in a race.

Amber stepped delicately around a clump of cactus, stopped, and whinnied softly. A low nicker answered her.

Linda listened intently. Just ahead, a steep, rocky slope blocked her view. She felt uneasy. The piles of rock all around were favorite places for rattlesnakes. She stared at the ground, straining her ears for any telltale rattle. The muscles in her neck tensed. Linda hated snakes—especially rattlers. Their bite could be deadly—even to a horse.

Then she heard the *clop* of a hoof on rock. She glanced up and saw Snowbird, his head lowered, right in front of them. But there was still no sign of Larry.

As she slid out of the saddle, Bob and Kathy caught up with her.

"Where's Larry?" Bob said, an anxious frown on his face.

"I don't know," Linda said grimly. She approached Snowbird cautiously—she didn't want to get nipped by the ornery Appaloosa. But it was as if Snowbird was happy to see them.

He stood still, looking almost humble. Then she saw what the trouble was—his reins were tangled in a clump of mesquite.

Bob and Kathy hurried over. "I'll lead him behind Rocket," Bob said, untangling the reins. "He might run off if you turn him loose."

Linda remounted. "Let's find Larry," she told Amber.

"He must have been thrown or something," Kathy said. "Maybe that earthquake set off a little landslide."

Now that Amber had found Snowbird, she stood still. Even when Linda urged her forward, she wouldn't budge.

Linda scanned the rocks at the foot of the mesa. Then she gasped. "I—I think I've found Larry."

About fifteen feet up the steep side of the mesa was a huge rock. And sticking out from behind it, still and unmoving, was a scuffed brown boot.

9 ♦♦♦♦

Bob scrambled up the slope on his hands and knees, Linda and Kathy right behind him. He bent over his friend anxiously. "Larry! Are you hurt? Are you all right?"

Slowly Larry opened his eyes. He was sprawled at an angle. The huge rock pinned down his leg. "What?"

"Is his leg broken?" Linda said.

Carefully Bob shifted the rock. He whistled. "Whew, that's a relief. It was just holding down the leg of his jeans."

"What happened?" Larry asked faintly.

"There was an earthquake," Linda said.

"That's right." Larry lifted himself up on one

elbow and winced. "Yeah, I remember. Snowbird got thrown off-balance. Where is he?"

"His reins got caught in some brush," Linda said. "He's fine. Amber heard him whinny so we knew where to find you."

Larry got up, with Bob helping. "I lost Eric. I figured I'd just ride a little way up the mesa—to get a better view of the area."

Bob helped Larry down the hill. When they were on their way home, Bob said, "I think we'd better leave this whole thing to Bronco and Doña, before one of us gets hurt. We aren't getting anywhere, crawling around in caves."

"I'm pretty sore," Larry admitted. "I don't think I'll be riding for a few days."

Linda rode in disappointed silence. She could understand Bob's being fed up, after everything that had happened. But she was more determined than ever to find that deed. She couldn't stand the thought of losing the ranch. If the others gave up, she'd go on alone.

Then Linda remembered Eric Danner and what he'd said. What other "tricks" did Silas Danner have up his sleeve? Bronco and Doña had to be warned.

But when they got back to the ranch house, Bronco and Doña weren't there. Neither was Mac. They were all in town, with the lawyers. And even when they came back, they spent a long time in Bronco's office, talking on the phone.

Linda and Bob didn't have a chance to talk to their grandparents until supper. Bronco was cooking steaks on the patio barbecue—and he didn't want to talk about his day.

"Wait till we tell you what happened to us," Linda said. "Mr. Danner had a spy on the ranch—and we found him."

"What do you mean?" Bronco asked.

"His grandson, Eric, has been spying on us," Bob explained. "He was in the stable yesterday, and he was following us out on the trail. When we caught him, he told us his grandfather wants the ranch for himself."

"And Eric says he's going to get it, too!" Linda cut in. "He says Mr. Danner has tricks he hasn't even tried yet."

Bronco frowned as he took in this news. "How did all this happen?" he asked.

"It's a long story," Linda explained. "Remember

that songbook we found in the trunk? There was this one song called 'The Golden Secret.' " She repeated the old song:

" 'My Children, where the coyote sings,
Find my Treasure, in the dark and cold.
Where my Shadow roamed, 'neath golden rings,
With my Treasure safe, I need no gold.' "

Bronco and Doña both looked mystified, but Linda went on. "We think it's a kind of code—telling that the deed might be hidden in one of Don Carlos's old gold mines."

Linda explained the clues she'd found in the words of the song.

"That's clever," Bronco said. "But I have a feeling you're pushing too hard—even for Don Carlos, full of ideas as he was."

"But otherwise the words don't make sense," Linda replied.

"To us," Bob said. "Maybe we just don't get it."

"You kids didn't go into those mines, did you?" Doña's face was full of concern. "That's dangerous!"

Bob and Linda both glanced at each other, a little

embarrassed. "We did, but we were careful," Bob explained. "We tied ourselves together, and Kathy stayed outside. She could have gone for help if we needed it."

"I don't want you going in those caves alone," Doña said. "Any more exploring you do should be done with an adult. Maybe Mac could go along."

"But—" Linda started to say.

"No buts," her grandfather said. "Some of those mines haven't been looked at in fifty years. You could get lost or hurt, or even killed."

Linda looked pleadingly at her grandparents. "All right. But we'd better start looking soon. If the deed is really hidden in one of them . . ."

"Right now, I'm more interested in those dirty tricks Eric mentioned," said Bronco.

Bob and Linda recounted everything that Eric had said, but it really wasn't much.

Everyone was just picking at their food when Mac came in, looking serious. "I found out about those two guys the kids met out on the range," he said. From the look on his face, it wasn't good news.

"The sheriff checked that license number you got off their pickup. It belongs to a couple of oil prospectors who do a lot of work for Silas Danner and his bank. I think they were checking out our land for signs of oil."

Linda got up. "Could I be excused?" she asked. Then she went out the door with Mac, her mind a whirl of worries.

So Eric was right. Silas Danner did want the ranch for himself, not for a cattle company, as he'd said. He was going to tear up Rancho del Sol to dig for oil. And he was so sure his land grab would go through, he had his men on the ranch already.

"Hey, hey." Mac's voice cut into her thoughts. "I didn't mean to upset you. Your folks won't take this lying down."

"Oh, Mac," Linda burst out, "we've got to help them!" The whole story of the day's adventure came tumbling out—along with the way Bronco and Doña had reacted to it.

Mac listened quietly, taking everything in. When Linda finished, he led the way to his office. "Cheer up!" he said. "They didn't come out and say, 'No exploring!' They just want somebody to go with you. And I'll do that. If that deed's out there to be found, we'll find it."

"Thanks, Mac. I just can't stand the thought of Eric Danner living on this ranch."

Mac shook his head. "I know what you mean. If the Danners got this place, I'd be shaking the dust of Rancho del Sol off my boots pretty quick!"

"It won't happen," Linda insisted. "That deed is out there somewhere—I just know it."

"Tell me those lines in the song again, will you?" Mac listened carefully, frowning in thought. "I wonder if he was talking about one of the caves where he didn't find *any* gold? That one you were in today yielded about the most they found on the ranch."

"I was thinking that, too. If there was a cave where they didn't find any gold, no one would be interested in it. Then the deed would be safer. People wouldn't be coming and going in there. But how do we know which one?"

Mac pulled open his file cabinet and flipped through some papers. "This should help," he said, pulling out a folded sheet.

"What is it?"

He spread out the paper. "There was an old map among Don Carlos's papers here in the desk. It was falling apart, so I made a copy, best as I could. You

can see here where he marked the mines that showed gold and the ones that didn't." He handed it to
her.

Linda looked at the map, which was dotted with
marks. She tapped an X. "This is where we were
today. And here's another X. But what's this O
supposed to mean?"

"Best as I can tell, each X is a mine where he found
gold. I think he put an O where he dug and *didn't*
find anything." Mac smiled. "He did it up real fancy,
marking every mine in gold ink."

Linda looked up. "The circles, too?"

Mac nodded.

"That line from 'The Golden Secret'—"'neath
golden rings'—maybe it was supposed to lead to this
map." She ran her finger along the map, finding an
O. "Golden circles—golden rings. He was telling his
children that the deed was in an empty mine!"

"Could be," Mac agreed.

Trying to hold down her excitement, Linda
searched for every O on the map. "We could start
with this one, over near the stream. Then we can
work around, back toward the house."

"It's a good idea," Mac said, "and it makes sense

to do it systematically. I'll get a couple of the hands to come with us and help. That mine's a long way from anywhere."

"What time should we leave? I'll get up first thing in the morning!"

Mac smiled. "As soon as you're ready, just come in here and get me."

Linda studied the map. "Mac, can I borrow this? I want to figure out the quickest way to get all of these explored."

"Sure, just be careful. I've got the original tucked away. You take the copy, but don't lose it. I don't want to have to make another one."

"Thanks, Mac. I'll be careful," Linda promised.

She was getting up from her seat as Bob came in. "Mac, you're needed at the house—right now. We've just found out about one of Danner's dirty tricks. He's pushing for a hearing this week—while Judge Braxton is in court."

"Braxton!" Mac looked as if he had tasted something bad. "He's an old pal of Danner's. I'll bet Silas would like to have this case decided by his golf buddy."

Doña and Bronco stayed up late, talking about the

latest development. From her bedroom, where she lay staring into the darkness, Linda could hear the murmur of their voices.

Sleep was a long time coming. A voice in her head kept repeating, *We've got to be right this time. We've got to find the deed!*

10 ♦♦♦♦

The next morning Linda woke up before sunrise. She got dressed, hurried through breakfast, and then headed off to Mac's office.

"All set, Mac," she said, peeking in through the open door. "When do we leave for those mines?"

Mac looked up from his desk, where he was stacking papers into a large pile. "I'm sorry, but it's going to have to wait until the day after tomorrow. I've got to go to town."

He tapped the stack in front of him. "This hearing thing has everyone running around. Bronco wants me to take these to our lawyers—personally. Then I've got to go dig around in the county records. I won't be back before noon."

"Mac . . ." Linda's voice trailed off in disappointment.

Mac shook his head. "Sorry, Linda. I know how much you want to get started, but this is important, too."

Linda just nodded, afraid to trust herself to say anything. She watched Mac square up the corners of the pile of papers and put them in a box. Then he got up with the box and headed for the ranch pickup. He waved good-bye with a smile, and Linda waved unhappily back.

It just wasn't fair! She knew she could find the deed if she could only get to the mines. Time was running out, but here she was, stuck because she didn't have a baby-sitter! Linda stomped her way into the stable. She couldn't remember ever feeling so frustrated.

Amber stirred in her stall and nickered a hello. When Linda came over, the mare nudged at her shoulder. In spite of her feelings, Linda smiled. "Want to get out, do you? Want to go for a ride?"

That's when the idea came to her. Even if Mac was busy, *she* had lots of time. She could at least ride over to that farthest mine and check it out. See if it had caved in or something. And if it looked all right, well, maybe she might take a look inside. *Maybe.*

For a moment, Linda thought about asking Bob to go with her, then decided not to. He'd probably call it a wild-goose chase. Or worse, ride out and then say, "Oh, it's not here. Let's go home."

Besides, she had to be back by noon or Mac would figure out where she had gone. Linda had enough to worry about without getting in trouble for disobeying her grandparents.

The early-morning air was cool. As Linda rode off, she felt as if she and Amber were the only creatures awake in the universe. The ranch was the whole world, and it stretched out in all directions as far as she could see. She let Amber run.

After a while the sun began to heat up the morning. There was no breeze, so she slowed Amber.

"It's going to be hot," she said.

Amber flicked her ears.

"It's *weather* weather. That's what Mac calls these kind of days." She squinted up into the sky. "It's sunny and hot now, but I'll bet you it'll be really cold tonight." Linda patted Amber on the neck. "But we don't have to worry. We'll be back home before anything happens."

She checked her shirt pocket to make sure the map was still folded inside and rode on.

From time to time she looked back to make sure no one was following her, although Bob wouldn't be up for at least another hour. He liked to sleep late.

She slowed Amber to a walk. The sun was climbing in the cloudless sky. Linda felt as if it would burn her finger if she reached out and touched it, like the electric burners on the stove.

"Today it's our sun," she told Amber. "Our ranch, our caves, our everything. Just you and me, Amber, you and me."

Amber tossed her head.

She speeded up to a trot and then eased into a slow, smooth, comfortable lope. Linda let her go at her own speed. Amber's gait was so easy, she felt as if she could ride clear across the world and not get tired.

They still had a long way to go, and after a while she slowed Amber down. Linda tipped her hat forward to protect her face from the sun. Overhead a hawk circled lazily, riding some air current that Linda couldn't feel.

Linda fanned herself with her hat. "I don't know about you, Amber. But I could go for a little breeze."

That was when they heard a muffled *whump!* beyond the next rise. Linda reined Amber in, then swung down out of the saddle. Another *whump!* cut through the silence, and Amber skittered nervously.

"Quiet down," Linda whispered. "This isn't an earthquake. I'm going to find out what it is."

She took off her hat and peeked over the top of the rise. Below her was a jeep, with two familiar characters standing beside it—the oil prospectors they'd run into two days earlier.

The prospectors had new equipment set up. One man stood before something that looked like a computer with a large screen. The other man was setting something up on the ground some distance away. He returned to the computer, and then came another *whump!*

Linda realized what the machine was. She'd seen one on TV. It used the sound waves from the small explosions to chart what was underground.

But the two prospectors weren't looking at their screen. They were looking up at the ridge, right at Linda. No, *behind* her.

Linda turned to see Amber rearing up on her hind legs, the whites of her eyes showing. Those explosions had made her nervous—and she'd made herself visible to the prospectors.

Now the two men were running up the rise. Linda jumped to her feet and ran back to her horse. "Amber! Here!"

Amber whinnied and trotted over to her. Linda grabbed the saddle horn and swung up into the saddle. She could hear the prospectors shouting.

With the reins in her hands, she wheeled Amber around and began galloping away.

Glancing back over her shoulder, Linda saw the two men heading back down the rise. She breathed a sigh of relief. Then she heard the jeep engine roaring into life.

Leaning forward in the saddle, she whispered into Amber's ear, "Let's get out of here." Amber tossed her head and put on more speed.

The jeep came tearing over the ridge, bouncing over the ground after them. Amber pushed herself even faster, but the jeep gained on them.

Linda realized there was no way they could outrun the machine. She'd have to lead them somewhere the jeep couldn't follow. She pulled on the reins, leading a zigzag course through some rocks and cacti.

It wasn't enough. The jeep was able to sweep ahead of them, nearly cutting them off.

Desperately, Linda pulled on the reins, and Amber darted around. They rode for the foothills, shimmering in front of them like a mirage. Only in that rough country did they have a chance to lose the jeep.

Ahead of them was a dry streambed, winding its way up into the hills. The ground was full of loose rocks, and Amber had to slow down.

Behind them, though, they could hear the jeep bouncing its way ever closer. Amber whinnied and flung herself forward.

The rocky walls of the cut were closing in now, as the streambed led upward. Just a little farther, and there'd be no room for the jeep. Would they make it?

Linda leaned forward across Amber's neck, whispering encouragement. A screech of metal on rock came from behind them. The jeep had gotten hung up on one of the walls.

Amber whinnied in triumph as she made her way up the rocky ground. Linda looked over her shoulder. The jeep was indeed stuck. One man was gunning the engine while the other pushed against the hood.

Linda and Amber jogged on into the hills. As soon

as they were out of sight of the two prospectors, Linda leaned forward and whispered, "Good girl, Amber," into the horse's ear. Amber whinnied with pleasure and plunged ahead. Soon they came to a small stream.

Linda stopped and led Amber to the bank. While the mare drank, Linda looked over her copy of Don Carlos's old map. After the wild chase, it was hard to figure out exactly where they were. But it looked as though an abandoned mine was nearby.

Linda walked around, searching the hillside for holes that could be caves. She checked her map again. It showed a cave close to a stream and beside a large boulder.

Linda picked up a stick and used it to poke at piles of rock that could hide the opening. She worked her way forward until she saw a boulder that could be the one shown on the map. She scooped away the dead brush piled up beside it. "Look, Amber, there's an opening! Maybe this is it!"

Amber came over and pawed at the hole lazily, as if she were digging. Then she went back to nibbling quietly at the dried grass.

"Well, I'll just take a quick look inside." Linda

crouched down and felt her way into the dark cave. It seemed a little bigger than the one she'd explored with Bob and Larry.

"Here goes nothing," Linda whispered. She took the flashlight from her belt and flicked the switch. This cave was higher. She'd have to crouch, but she could walk on two feet, instead of crawling along. Behind her, Linda heard Amber paw at the entrance. "Take it easy," she called back.

Linda moved slowly, playing the light on both sides, looking for any place where a deed could have been left. How big would a deed be? It would have to be in something to protect it—maybe another saddle-bag.

Outside, Amber whinnied. It must have upset her to see Linda disappear into the earth.

After a few moments, Linda stopped. This is it—I've gone far enough, she decided. Her back hurt from not being able to straighten up. Just as she started to turn, though, she stubbed her toe on something.

She aimed the light at the floor. What was it? A rock? The thing was so encrusted with dirt, she couldn't tell what it was. But whatever it was, it wasn't a rock. It was too angular. Linda quickly scooped it up—it was some kind of box—and started back toward the cave mouth.

She couldn't wait to be back in the sunshine. And it wasn't just for light to examine the box she'd found. It was chilly in the dark cave. She remembered Don Carlos's song—"in the dark and cold"—and shivered. That line was exactly right.

Linda hurried, coughing in the musty, dead air of the cave. She couldn't move too quickly, though. If she did, she might hit her head on one of the timbers that held up the roof.

As she moved, Linda could hear the timbers creaking from time to time. They hadn't done that on the way in—had they? What if a timber gave way? She wanted to be out of there—now!

After a while the darkness seemed to be turning gray. She shut off the flashlight to see if she had imagined it. No, she could see a faint, irregularly shaped paleness ahead—the entrance to the tunnel. Thank goodness. She was almost there.

A noise came to her from outside—Amber's whinny?

"Calm down, Amber, I'm coming," Linda called.

But her words were drowned out by a deep rumbling in the tunnel. "Oh, no—not now!" Linda cried.

She tried to move faster, but nearly fell to her knees as the earth shook with a sharp tremor.

A timber overhead cracked. Rocks and dirt showered down on her. Linda still tried to press on but flinched back as, with a huge crash, something fell right in front of her.

She reached forward in the darkness to find a huge boulder completely blocking the tunnel.

She was trapped!

11 ◆◆◆◆

Linda threw herself at the boulder, trying to push it out of her way, but it wouldn't move. She stepped back, panting in the darkness. What should she do? She had dropped the flashlight when the rock fell. Frantically, she knelt and groped around until she found it.

Even as she flicked the switch, she knew the flashlight wasn't going to work. She'd heard the faint tinkle of glass when she'd picked it up. The bulb was broken.

Then, as her eyes got accustomed to the darkness, she realized there was a very faint, ghostly glimmer in the air. The boulder cut off most but not all of the light coming in from outside. She could see enough to make things out.

Cautiously, she touched the timber crossbeam overhead to make sure it was still in place. It creaked ominously. If that timber gave way, she would be buried under tons of rock and dirt.

Once again she tried with all her strength to push the boulder, but it didn't budge. Linda leaned against the rock, shaking.

Then a sound came from the mouth of the cave. "Is someone there?" she called. "Bob? Is it you? I'm trapped."

There was no answer, but she heard the sound again. This time she recognized it—a horse's hoof, pawing at the earth. It was Amber, trying to get to her! At least she wasn't alone!

Linda sagged against the rock again. Smart as Amber was, she couldn't dig all the dirt away, or move the boulder.

Linda had been around horses long enough to know that, once free, they generally returned to their stable. Amber was her only hope.

"Go home, Amber!" Linda called through the small opening. "Go get help!" Linda knew how much her horse loved her, and she was afraid Amber might not leave her there alone.

She heard Amber neigh. It was a comforting

sound, just to know she was out there. But then the sound stopped.

Only then did Linda realize that she was still clutching the old box in her hand. She wished she had at least looked inside. What if I've actually found the deed and then gotten myself stuck in here? she thought.

Right now, though, she had another use for the box. Digging with that and the handle of the broken flashlight, she started clearing away the dirt that had fallen with the boulder. She didn't think she could dig the huge stone out, but maybe it would make it easier to move the rock when help came.

In her mind, Linda could see Amber arriving back at the barn without her. Mac would realize something was wrong and come out to help. Oh no! Mac was the only one who might figure out where she had gone—and he was in town until at least noon.

Desperately, Linda tried digging around the boulder, but it stayed where it was. It was just too heavy for her to move it alone.

The overhead timbers continued to creak, and dirt and stones kept falling from the mine's ceiling. If the earthquake had weakened the mine shaft, it might all come down at any moment. With each loud creak,

Linda held her breath. But after a few moments, things got quiet again, and she sighed with relief.

After a while, Linda slumped tiredly down to the ground, leaning against the cave wall.

A sudden sound made her skin crawl. Was that the hiss of a snake? She remembered the snake that had slithered under her hand in the other cave. There were rattlers in these hills. What if one was trapped in here with her? Linda didn't know if snakes could see in the dark or not. But she did know what would happen if the snake found her. With as little movement as possible, she curled her body up into a small ball.

Bronco was right, she told herself miserably. These mines are dangerous. She should never have ridden off by herself. It could be hours—or even days—until help came. All she could do was wait.

It seemed as if she'd been stuck in the cave forever. Curled up in the darkness, Linda lost all track of time. She closed her eyes, trying to think of anything she could do. It was cold, and she was so tired. All her muscles were starting to ache from being cramped up underground.

Linda didn't know when she dozed off, but she

woke up with a start. Had she been dreaming? Or had she really heard a metallic *ping?* Then it came again. Linda pulled herself up, forcing stiff muscles to work. She listened for the noise, then realized she was hearing muffled voices. Help had come! They must be digging outside!

After a few minutes, the voices grew fainter. Then the noise stopped. Were they giving up? Were they going to look in another cave? Linda couldn't let them leave.

"Help!" she screamed. "It's me! I'm in here!"

She clawed her way into the small space at the top of the boulder. "Don't go away, I'm in here!"

Then she heard an answering shout, and the digging continued. She couldn't understand what they were saying. It was enough for her to know that they were out there.

Then Mac's voice came through loud and clear. "Linda, can you hear me? You aren't hurt, are you?" he said.

"No, no. I'm okay."

"All right. Looks like we've got a big rock to get out of the way. Bob, hand me a rope."

Linda could hear Bob's voice in the background.

Then something cool touched her hands. She gasped, then realized it was only the handle of Mac's flashlight. "Hold this steady if you can, honey, so I can see to get the rope around this thing. Bob, tell Larry to tie the rope to the jeep so we can move this rock out of the way. I'll give him the signal to start."

A few moments later she heard Larry calling, "All set out here, Mac."

"All right. Start up the jeep, real slow. You go too fast, boy, and you'll pull that rock right over me. I want you to stop every few feet and check us out. Got it?"

Linda heard the roar of the jeep as the ignition caught. Seconds later, the heavy rock began to move, scraping along the floor of the cave. She could hear Mac saying, "Easy, easy, not too fast. Bob, mind that rope."

As far as Linda was concerned, Mac's voice, the roar of the old jeep, and Amber's neigh were the most beautiful sounds she'd ever heard.

When the rock was finally out of the tunnel, Mac leaned in to get her. Gently, he helped her out of the cave and into the warm sunshine. Larry and Bob rushed to her.

Amber was there, too, nosing her way to Linda with a little whinny. Linda couldn't hold back the tears that flooded her eyes.

In spite of the warm sunshine, Linda was shivering. Mac got a blanket from the back of the jeep, wrapped it around her, and lifted her onto the seat. Bob poured hot cider from a thermos.

"Amber came tearing home without you," Bob said. "We were really worried, since nobody knew where you'd gone."

"So they called me, in town," Mac said. "I had a pretty good idea where you might be."

"Then Amber led us back here—right to you!" Larry added.

"Without her, we'd have wasted a lot of time looking in empty holes," Mac said. "That is one great horse!"

"If it weren't for her . . ." Bob paused, knowing he'd been wrong about Amber. "You're lucky to have her, Linda."

Linda sat in the jeep wrapped in the blanket while Mac and the boys recovered the rope. Amber came over to watch her and nuzzled Linda's hair.

"Amber, you saved my life." Linda reached up and

held Amber's head to her own, giving her a big hug. Then she remembered the box, still clutched in her other hand.

Bob came to stand near her as she shook the box, sending loose dirt dribbling through a hole in the top. "Hey, what have you got there?" he asked.

"I found it in the cave." She shook it again. "I think there's something inside."

"Probably dirt." Bob grinned. "It looks like an old tobacco tin."

Linda started to throw the box away, but stopped. She took the key out of the jeep's ignition and used it to scrape away some of the crusted silt at the bottom of the can. "Bob?"

He came quickly. "What's wrong?"

She handed him the can. "There *is* something in here."

Larry and Mac gathered around as Bob very carefully removed a piece of paper folded over and over until it was very small.

"We're going to feel pretty stupid if this is just an ad for chewing tobacco," Larry joked.

Bob unfolded the paper with great care. The creases had been made so long ago, they were in danger of tearing. When he got the paper unfolded, he stared at it and gasped.

"What is it?" Linda asked.

Bob handed it to her, solemn-faced. "Read for yourself."

Slowly Linda read the old-fashioned script aloud:

"KNOW ALL MEN BY THESE PRESENTS, THAT I, GOVERNOR OF THE STATE OF CALIFORNIA, IN CONSIDERATION OF SERVICES RENDERED TO THIS STATE BY DON CARLOS PEREZ, DO HEREBY AC-KNOWLEDGE AND DO RELEASE QUITCLAIM UNTO THE SAID DON CARLOS PEREZ, HIS HEIRS, AND HIS ASSIGNS FOREVER THE ACRES BOUND ON THE WEST BY——"

A triumphant yell stopped her. "Well, all right," Mac said. "All *right*."

Larry gave a wild "Wahoo!" and did a handspring.

"You did it!" Bob said. "You found the deed!"

Linda beamed. Amber came over and nuzzled her pocket, looking for a piece of sugar. "Well, I couldn't have done it without Amber!"

She climbed out of the jeep, unwrapping the

blanket, and swung up onto Amber's back. "Come on, we've got to get back with the good news!"

As she set off, Linda was still a little stiff from having been cramped in the cave. But she quickly settled into Amber's gait. The heat of the sun felt friendly. And she was warm inside, as well—with triumph, for finding the deed when everyone else had given up. But she also felt relief that their worries were over—and pride, for what she and Amber had done.

Linda let Amber out into a slow, smooth trot. Then, as the ranch house came into view, they broke into a gallop. Linda's hat went sailing off, and her hair streamed behind her in the breeze.

They thundered along the path to the house, and up to the patio, where Doña, Bronco, and Luisa all stood.

Doña gasped when she saw Linda charging up, still covered with dust from the mine. "Linda! What happened? Are you okay?"

Linda smiled. "I'm better than okay, Doña. I have something for you!" She swung off the saddle, reaching into her shirt pocket.

Doña and Bronco gently spread out the paper she

gave them. Together they looked at the deed, their eyes shining with relief.

Doña walked over to Linda and gave her a hug. "Thank you, darling. I can't believe this—where did you find it?"

But Bronco's eyes were sharper as he looked at Linda. "You disobeyed me, didn't you? You went in the caves."

Linda nodded. "I'm sorry, Bronco. I know—" She was interrupted by the arrival of the jeep. Bob, Larry, and Mac, all talking at the same time, began telling the story of her disaster in the cave and how Amber helped save her.

"Honey, I'm glad you found the deed. You saved the ranch." Doña hugged her again. "But you could have been hurt."

Then, with her arm still around her granddaughter, Doña turned toward the house. "I think what you need now is a good hot bath."

"And we need a celebration!" Bronco said. "Tomorrow we'll show the deed to Danner. For tonight —how about a barbecue?"

Luisa chimed in from the doorway. "I'll have homemade ice cream and chocolate cake and burritos and . . . you name it, I'll make it! Anything you want!"

Teasing Luisa, Linda said, "Can Amber come to the party?"

Luisa grinned. "Today, I'll even let her into my kitchen."

"Before she visits with you, she needs a walk to cool down. Don't worry, Linda. Larry and I will take care of her, won't we, Larry?" Bob said.

"You bet! Today Amber gets anything she wants, too!"

Linda came downstairs feeling clean, rested, and happy. They'd won! They'd keep the ranch! The look on Doña's face when Linda had given her the deed had been worth ten times as much trouble as Linda had gone through.

No one was in the house, but she heard voices outside, and the cooking smells wafting in made her remember how hungry she was.

Everyone was out on the patio. Not only Doña and Bronco and Bob and Mac, but Larry and Kathy and their parents, and nearly all of the ranch hands. There were big vases of fresh flowers, and Mac's tape deck was playing lively music.

As Linda came out, everyone crowded around to congratulate her. Mac stepped away, to come back leading Amber, wearing a necklace made of bright flowers.

"Looks like she just won the Kentucky Derby," Bob said.

"Better than that," Bronco said. "She and Linda won us our ranch."

As he was speaking, a car pulled up, and Silas Danner got out. He stopped in surprise, not expecting to find a party going on. "I came by for one last discussion before we went to court," he said. "But if this isn't the time . . ."

"Oh, this is *exactly* the time," Bronco said. "And it *will* be the last discussion." He held up the ancient piece of paper. "You know what this is? A deed —issued to Don Carlos Perez."

Danner jumped back as if he'd seen a ghost.

"We did some checking, getting ready for the hearing, and we know that there's no cattle company. We know *you* wanted our ranch for the oil and mineral rights. But the ranch is ours—and you won't be tearing it up."

Silas Danner said, "Now, Bronco . . . I hope you won't do anything foolish. . . ."

Bronco laughed. "Nothing foolish. But I do have a party going on—a deed celebration."

Everyone was silent as Danner quickly left.

Then Bob called out, "Three cheers for Linda! Hip, hip . . ."

"Hooray!" everyone shouted.

"I think the cheers should be for someone else," Linda said, putting her arm around Amber's neck. "Without her, I wouldn't be here—and neither would the deed."

"Well, I have something Amber would like better than cheers!" Luisa picked up the silver sugar bowl, and not letting herself have time to be scared, she marched up to Amber and held it out to her. "You deserve it," she said.

But when Amber leaned forward to grab the cubes, Luisa shrieked, dropped the sugar bowl on the patio floor, and hurriedly backed away. Then she began laughing at herself, and everyone joined in.

Linda picked up the sugar and gave some to Amber, who nickered.

"She says thank you, Luisa," Linda said. Then she put her head against Amber's neck. "You're a hero now, Amber. Nobody will ever doubt you again."